THE CLEVERNESS OF MR. BUDD

Solicitor Larry Graham drives urgently to the Yorkshire Moors home of a client, Benjamin Starl, who is gravely ill. Starl's secretary, Margaret Lane, shows Larry to his bedroom, but his client has been brutally murdered — a knife embedded in his body! Then, Superintendent Budd from Scotland Yard arrives and discovers the dead body of a strangled man lying on the steps outside . . . And in *The Black Widow*, Budd's hunt for stolen jewellery turns into a murder investigation of foggy Dartmoor.

GERALD VERNER

THE CLEVERNESS OF MR. BUDD

Complete and Unabridged

LINFORD
Leicester

First published in Great Britain

First Linford Edition
published 2011

British Library CIP Data

Verner, Gerald.
  The cleverness of Mr. Budd.- -
  (Linford mystery library)
  1. Budd, Robert (Fictitious character)- -
  Fiction. 2. Detectives- - England- -Fiction.
  3. Murder- -Investigation- -England- -Fiction.
  4. Detective and mystery stories.
  5. Large type books.
  I. Title II. Series
  823.9′12–dc22

  ISBN 978–1–4448–0747–9

Published by
F. A. Thorpe (Publishing)
Anstey, Leicestershire

Set by Words & Graphics Ltd.
Anstey, Leicestershire
Printed and bound in Great Britain by
T. J. International Ltd., Padstow, Cornwall

This book is printed on acid-free paper

1

THE WHISPERING MAN

1

Wanted!

Joe Altman was an Englishman by birth and an American by force of circumstances. When, under the watchful eyes of the men from Scotland Yard who were looking for him, Mr. Altman walked up the gangway to board a Cunard liner at Southampton, his appearance was so altered that even his greatest friend, Luke Kelland, would not have recognized him. He was more like an American than the real ones among his fellow-passengers.

Joe could not be good, but at least he was careful, and his get-away had been methodically planned.

He left the shores of England with the newspapers ringing with his name — and with ten notes for a thousand pounds each stitched into the lining of his jacket, that being the amount he had wrung from Solly Hartfeld in exchange for the

3

Thorndale Emeralds.

He spent the next three years in America and found them profitable, becoming almost as big a nuisance to the New York police as he had been to their London confreres. During this period he kept up a regular correspondence with his friend Kelland, and through him learned of the easiest coup of his life.

For a month he was very busy indeed. At the end of that time he left America for England, carrying with him, snugly concealed in the heel of one of his neat, carefully-polished shoes, the equivalent to several thousand pounds. And it was comfortably reassuring to know that there would be no kick coming from the man he had robbed, for the object he had stolen had been acquired by its previous possessor in a totally illegal way, and he would not dare to make his loss public.

An additional cause for satisfaction was that his market was ready and waiting. He had only to deliver the goods, receive the five thousand pounds he had been promised, and the whole thing would be over and done with.

Unfortunately for Mr. Altman, things did not work out quite so easily as he had anticipated. The first hitch occurred soon after his return to England, when the buyer, after locking his recent acquisition away in his safe, produced a cheque book and started to write out a cheque for the agreed amount. Mr. Altman, who had a constitutional distrust of cheques, bred from bitter experience, frowned, and stopped him.

'I'm not taking that,' he said decisively. 'I want cash!'

'Do you think I keep five thousand pounds in the house?' demanded his client harshly.

'I don't care whether you keep it in the house or not,' retorted Joe. 'You can get it!'

The hard-faced old man was silent for a moment, then he closed his cheque book and put it back in the drawer of his desk.

'All right,' he grunted ungraciously; 'come back tomorrow at the same time and I'll have cash for you.'

Mr. Altman went optimistically away,

full of schemes for the future, none of which was destined to be realized. For that night the second hitch occurred, and it was more serious than the first.

He had taken rooms at a small but select hotel near the Strand, and he was considering going to bed when there came a tap on his door. Without waiting for his permission, two men entered.

'You're registered as Hansen, but your name is Altman,' said the larger of the two authoritatively, 'I'm Superintendent Budd of Scotland Yard, and I want you in connection with the robbery of the Thorndale Emeralds!'

Joe argued and protested indignantly, but without creating any impression on his sceptical hearers.

He was hustled into a cab and driven to Scotland Yard, where they took his fingerprints to compare with those attached to his dossier. Then, if not before, he knew that argument was useless.

At the end of the short trial that followed in due course, he was sent down for five years, and the only comfort he possessed was the knowledge that five thousand pounds waited for him at the end of his sentence.

★ ★ ★

On the morning of the day following Mr. Altman's release, a little over four years later, Larry Graham, junior partner in the firm of Carlock, Carlock & Graham, solicitors, was rung up at his flat by Mr. Edward Carlock, the only other surviving member of the firm.

'I was hoping that I would catch you before you left for the office,' said Mr. Carlock, in his dry, precise voice. 'I'm afraid I shall not be able to get there today. My lumbago is worse, and it would be foolhardy to venture out in this weather. Can you attend to everything?'

'Of course,' answered Larry, who was used to these periodical absences of his partner. 'Is there anything of particular importance?'

'No.' Mr. Carlock mentioned a list, no item of which could be called important by any stretch of the imagination. Larry sympathised with the lawyer over his ailment, cut short a threatened discourse on lumbago in general and Mr. Carlock's variety in particular, and went back to his interrupted breakfast.

He was a good-looking man of thirty-five, but looked ten years younger, with the build of an athlete, and few people would have guessed his profession from his appearance.

He reached the old-fashioned offices in Lincoln's Inn as the clocks were striking nine, and found that far from there being nothing of importance there was something that was very important indeed. The grey-haired head clerk met him with the information that an urgent telephone message had just arrived for Mr. Carlock.

'It's from Mr. Starl, sir,' said the old man. 'He wants Mr. Carlock to go and see him at once. Mr. Starl has been taken suddenly ill and is not expected to live.'

Larry frowned and pursed his lips. Benjamin Starl, the millionaire, was one of their oldest and most valued clients.

'Mr. Carlock's not coming in today, Andrews,' he said, 'so I'll have to attend to this. Mr. Starl lives in Yorkshire, doesn't he?'

Andrews nodded.

'Yes, sir; near Lastingham. The house is on the edge of Lastingham Moor. I've never been there myself, but Mr. Carlock told me that it was a very lonely place. Moorland Lodge it's called, and it's the only house for miles.'

'Sounds a nice cheerful place to get to,' said Larry, with a grimace and, going into his office, rang up the senior partner to acquaint him with the news.

At ten minutes to ten he climbed into his car and set off through pouring rain on his long journey, having arranged with Andrews to telephone Benjamin Starl and notify him of his impending arrival. And beside him, unseen as he drove through the drizzle and murk of that October day, sat the shadow of death!

2

The whispering man

It was dark when Larry brought his car to a halt at the gates of Moorland Lodge and got stiffly out into the driving rain. The roadway was a slippery morass of semi-liquid mud, and his feet sank in it almost to his ankles as he stood beside the car and took stock of his surroundings.

It had rained heavily ever since he had left London, and looked as if it would continue to do so throughout the coming night.

Around him stretched a desolate expanse of open moorland, across which the wind came fitfully in cold, biting gusts that penetrated his heavy overcoat and made him shiver. He turned and, in the light of the car's lamps, inspected the entrance to the house of the man he had come to see.

High wooden gates set in a wall of crumbling grey stone shut out all sight of the drive to the house. It was more like the entrance to a factory than a private residence. Not the sort of place one would expect a millionaire to live in, he decided.

He went over to the closed gates and searched for a bell-pull, but all he found was a heavy iron ring-latch. Twisting this, he found that the gates were not locked. He fastened them back, and after a little manoeuvring in the slippery mud, succeeded in running his car into the dark tunnel of the drive. Then, reclosing the gates, he continued towards the house, finally sighting it after rounding a sharp bend.

It was a square, ugly building of the same cold, grey stone as the wall that encircled it. A light burned in a glass transom above the massive front door, and a pale glimmer shone from one of the upper windows. Otherwise, the place was in darkness.

There was another car drawn up near the entrance, and he had hardly stopped his own when the door opened and a man's figure appeared, silhouetted against the light from within. The man peered out into the darkness and then came halfway down the steps.

'Are you Mr. Graham, sir?' he asked, and his voice was a peculiar tense whisper — clear enough, but like the voice of someone suffering from acute laryngitis.

Larry slid out from behind the wheel on to the circular sweep of gravel in front of the house.

'Yes,' he answered. 'How is Mr. Starl?'

'Very weak, sir,' came the reply, in the same strange whisper. 'He's been asking for you, sir, and is very anxious to see you at once. Have you any luggage?'

'Only a suitcase,' answered Larry.

'I'll attend to that, sir, and have the car taken round to the garage,' said the man who, from his dress, Larry concluded was the butler. 'If you will go into the hall — '

'Is that Mr. Graham, Dillon?' A low, soft voice broke in before the man could complete his sentence, and a girl came into the circle of light cast by the shaded hall-lamp.

She was small and slim, and her hair gleamed like sunlit honey as she stood under the hanging lamp, looking questioningly through the open doorway.

'Yes, miss,' replied the butler in his penetrating whisper, adding to Larry: 'This is Miss Lane, sir — Mr. Starl's secretary.'

Larry crossed the intervening strip of wet gravel and ascended the steps.

'I'm so glad you've come, Mr. Graham,' said the girl, as he entered the big, square hall. 'Mr. Starl has been getting rather anxious.'

She gave him an appraising glance, in which he detected a slight element of surprise and, guessing its cause, his eyes twinkled.

'Mr. Starl was taken ill very suddenly, wasn't he?' asked Larry, shedding his damp overcoat. 'What's the matter with him?'

'It's his heart. It has always troubled him, and yesterday he had a serious attack. Dr. Taplow says it is only a question of hours — ' She broke off as Dillon entered, carrying Larry's suitcase.

'I'll take this to the room which has been prepared for you, sir,' he said, 'and then arrange with the chauffeur about your car.'

'Thank you,' said Larry, and for the first time was able to get a good look at the man. At the first sound of that unpleasant, whispering voice he had taken an instinctive dislike to the butler, and the man's appearance only enhanced this impression.

The butler was tall and thin, with a long, sallow face, crowned by sparse strands of jet-black hair that only partially concealed an incipient baldness. His eyebrows were very bushy and grew unevenly, over-hanging his small, pale, restless eyes. His lips were thin and bloodless, and on the left side of his skinny neck, starting from the lobe of the ear and disappearing below the front of the collar, was an ugly scar.

Larry watched his ungainly figure ascending the stairs and thought he had seldom seen a more unprepossessing man.

As the butler disappeared in the shadows above, Larry became aware that the girl was looking at him curiously. He turned.

'Does he always talk in that funny whisper?' he asked, jerking his head towards the staircase.

'Dillon? Yes. He had some kind of an accident, I believe,' she replied. 'He's rather weird, isn't he?'

'Very,' replied Larry, though 'sinister' struck him as a better description.

'I don't like him,' she said. 'He's a very good butler, but there's something sneaky about him.'

A stout little man came hurrying down the stairs at that moment and trotted towards them.

'I'm going now, Miss Lane,' he said abruptly, giving Larry a quick, shrewd glance. 'But I'll be back later on tonight. There's nothing we can do except keep him quiet and avoid anything in the nature of excitement.'

'This is Dr. Taplow,' said Margaret, introducing the newcomer to Larry.

'How do you do?' said the little doctor, extending a plump hand and giving Larry a surprisingly strong grip.

'Glad to meet you, Mr. Graham. Mr. Starl has been asking for you repeatedly. He's a little stronger now, I'm glad to say, though I'm afraid — '

He pursed his lips, shook his round, grey head, and shrugged his shoulders, all in one concerted motion.

'You don't think he'll pull through?' asked Larry.

'I don't,' said the doctor candidly, struggling into his overcoat and winding a check muffler carefully around his throat. 'Advanced heart disease, you know. I've been expecting a collapse for years.' He picked up a hat and gloves. 'Well, goodbye for the present, Miss Lane. I'll be back in about three hours.'

He nodded to Larry and went out through the still open front door into the wet darkness of the night.

The girl went over and closed the door gently behind him,

'Now if you're ready, Mr. Graham,' she said, 'I'll take you up to Mr. Starl.'

Larry picked up the dispatch-case he had brought in with him and followed her up the heavily carpeted stairs. They came to a broad landing, dimly lighted, the same size as the hall below. To left and right ran a corridor, and as they turned into the left-hand passage the figure of the butler, Dillon, passed them, walking swiftly and noiselessly. The thickness of the carpet that covered the floor would have prevented his footsteps being heard, in any case, but there was something cat-like about the man's movements that Larry found particularly repellent.

Halfway down the corridor the girl stopped before a closed door and tapped softly. There was no reply. She tapped again. After a pause, when there was still no answer, she turned the handle softly and, pushing the door open, peered in.

Over her shoulder Larry caught a glimpse of a large, comfortably furnished bedroom. A shaded lamp stood on the table by the bed, and the light from a coal-fire flickered on the ceiling.

'I think Mr. Starl must have fallen asleep,' the girl whispered. 'If so, I won't disturb him. Wait here a moment, will you?'

He nodded, and she went softly into the room.

He saw her tiptoe over to the bed and peer down at its motionless occupant.

The scream she gave brought him quickly to her side.

'What is it?' he asked in alarm. 'What's the matter?'

With a face from which every vestige of colour had drained, she pointed at the bed.

'Look!' she whispered hoarsely.

At first Larry could see nothing to account for the horror in her eyes; the old man who lay there appeared to be sleeping. And then he saw, and caught his breath sharply. A red wet patch had oozed through the coverlet, and something was dripping from the bed to the floor.

Setting his teeth, Larry stepped closer to the bedside and pulled down the covers. And then he jerked back with a cry, for the sheets were crimson and horrible, and from the left side of Benjamin Starl, protruded the handle of a knife!

3

The visitor

Horror-struck, Larry gazed at the ghastly sight, then he hastily pulled the bed-clothes back to shut out the sight of the grim corpse and turned to the terrified girl.

'Go and fetch the doctor back,' he said sharply. 'Hurry, or you won't be in time to catch him!'

When she had gone Larry went back to the bed and stood looking down at the thin-faced old man who lay there.

Benjamin Starl was dead — it didn't require a doctor to tell him that. And he had been murdered!

Feeling a cold wind blow on the back of his neck, he saw for the first time that the window was open. Going over to it, he found that the lower sash had been raised some six inches. Pushing it right up, he leaned out.

The night was very dark and it was still raining heavily. He could hear the hiss of the downpour on the gravel below and feel the cool drops on his face. Against the sill rested the top of a ladder, and Larry's lips set in a thin line as he saw it. So the killer had come from without. He examined the floor below the window and found several damp smudges on the polished woodwork.

As he straightened up, a sound at the door made him turn, and he saw that Dillon was standing on the threshold.

'Was that Miss Lane who screamed, sir?' asked the butler anxiously, in his peculiar, whispering voice. 'What was the matter?'

'Your master has been murdered,' said Larry curtly. 'Miss Lane has gone to recall the doctor. I suppose you didn't hear anything when you were up here?'

'No, sir. I heard nothing.' Whatever shock Dillon had felt at the news had passed, and he was his normal self. 'I didn't come near this room sir.'

'But you were in the corridor,' said Larry. 'You passed Miss Lane and myself.'

'Yes, I was in the corridor,' said the man, nodding. 'The room that has been allotted to you, sir, is the next but one to Mr. Starl's. I had been there to leave your suitcase. I suppose there is no doubt, sir, that Mr. Starl is dead?'

'None whatever,' said Larry. 'Now go and telephone the police, will you?'

As the butler turned reluctantly away there came the sound of voices in the corridor and Dr. Taplow bustled into the room, followed by Margaret Lane. The little man's fat face had lost much of its colour.

'This is a shocking thing that Miss Lane tells me — shocking!' he said, speaking jerkily. His hurried ascent of the stairs had rendered him breathless. 'How did it happen?'

Larry briefly told him all he knew, and the doctor, nodding quickly, went over to the bed. He had reached out his hand to pull down the clothes when the young lawyer muttered something in his ear and, with a nod, the doctor turned.

'I don't think you'd better wait, Miss Lane,' he said quietly. 'It's not a very pleasant sight for a woman. We'll see you downstairs.'

The girl nodded and went out, leaving them alone with the dead man.

Taplov pulled back the bedclothes, and Larry heard his breath hiss sharply through his teeth as he saw the shambles that they had concealed. The next second he had recovered his professional calm and set about his examination rapidly and methodically. He was in the act of touching the hilt of the knife when Larry intervened.

'Be careful, Doctor,' he warned. 'There may be fingerprints.'

'H'm — yes, I suppose you're right.' muttered Taplow. 'Of course you are. Oh, well, we'll leave it where it is for the time being!' He continued his examination, and presently straightened up, wiping his face with his handkerchief. 'Rather horrible, isn't it? You say the murderer came from outside?'

'Apparently,' replied the young lawyer. 'There's a ladder against the window and several wet smudges on the floor beneath.'

He pointed them out to the little

doctor as he spoke.

'H'm!' muttered Taplow, and rubbed his double chin. 'He must have come in almost directly after I left. Pretty cool customer, don't you think?'

Before Larry could express his views there was a tap on the door, and Dillon entered.

'Excuse me, sir,' he said. 'But I can't get through to the police.'

'What do you mean, you can't get through to them?' demanded Larry. 'Isn't there any reply?'

'It isn't that, sir,' said the butler. 'I can't get any answer from the exchange. Something appears to have gone wrong with the telephone.'

Larry frowned. Following on the heels of the murder the sudden failure of the telephone had a significance that was not altogether pleasant. Was it an ordinary breakdown, or had the instrument been deliberately put out of action?

'Where is your telephone?' he asked abruptly.

'In Miss Lane's office, sir,' answered the butler, who had been watching him

23

closely. 'There's an extension in the Museum, but the main instrument is in Miss Lane's room.'

'The Museum?'

Larry looked at him questioningly, a little puzzled.

'Mr. Starl's study is called the Museum, sir, by the members of the household,' explained Dillon. 'The Chinese collection is housed there.'

It was then that Larry remembered the dead man's hobby.

'Oh, yes!' he said. 'I'll come down and have a look at that telephone, Dillon, and if you have such a thing as an electric torch in the house, would you mind bringing it to me?'

Going over to the window, he closed it and snapped the catch. Then the young lawyer took the key from the inside of the door, closed it behind them and locked it, putting the key in his pocket.

Dillon was waiting at the head of the stairs, and he led the way down and across the hall to a room on the right.

'This is Miss Lane's office, sir,' he said, opening the door.

It was a tiny apartment, furnished with a desk, a row of filing cabinets, and a small case of reference books. There was another door opposite the one they had entered, and beside a typewriter on the desk stood a telephone. Near it was a small, square box, fitted with a switch and an indicator.

'You press the switch down, sir, to put the connection through to the Museum,' explained Dillon. 'Otherwise this instrument is directly connected with the exchange.'

Larry nodded and picked up the telephone.

There was no sound from the earpiece. He tapped the switch bar for some time, but no voice answered.

Dropping the instrument back on its rack, he returned to the hall and began to trace the wires. From the little office they ran along one side of the hall to the front door, and from here passed outside the house. So far as he could see up to this point they were undamaged. If there had been any tampering it had been done outside.

'Get that torch I asked for, will you?' he said, and as Dillon turned away Margaret came out from a room facing the staircase.

Except that her face was deathly pale she was quite cool and collected.

'What are you looking for?' she asked curiously.

Larry told her.

'The telephone was all right early this evening,' she said, wrinkling her forehead. 'A man rang up asking to speak to Mr. Starl just before you arrived.'

'A friend of his?' asked Larry quickly.

She shook her head.

'I don't know who it was,' she answered. 'He wouldn't give his name. I told him Mr. Starl was very ill, and he rang off.'

'Why trouble about the telephone?' put in Dr. Taplow. 'I'm going to Lastingham, and I can notify the police if you like.'

'That's awfully good of you,' began Larry, but his words were waved away by a chubby hand.

'Not at all — not at all,' said the little man. 'Only too glad to do anything I can — ' He broke off suddenly, his head on one side, listening. 'Isn't that a car?' he asked.

Larry, who had heard the sound, too, nodded.

The sound of the approaching car grew louder and then stopped. A door slammed and a heavy footstep crunched on the wet gravel.

'Is that someone at the door, miss?'

The whispering voice of Dillon at his elbow made Larry start. The butler had joined them so silently that they had not heard his coming. He carried an electric torch in his hand, and he was breathing heavily, as though he had been hurrying. In the light from the hanging lamp his shoulders glistened, and Larry saw with surprise that his black coat was wet. The butler had evidently been out in the rain.

Before the girl could answer his question a sharp, authoritative knock came on the door. After a momentary hesitation, Dillon moved quickly forward, and twisting the heavy latch, pulled the door open.

The figure of a very large man loomed

out of the darkness. A veritable mountain of a man, whose bulk seemed to fill the big doorway.

'Good evenin'!' said a slow, sleepy voice. 'Perhaps somebody'll tell me — what this is doin' here?'

Larry saw the newcomer glance down at his feet, heard the butler's smothered exclamation and, going to Dillon's side, discovered the reason.

Sprawling limply on the steps was a man, and one glance at the dreadful face and staring eyes told Larry that he had been strangled!

4

Mr. Budd introduces himself

'Well?' said the fat man, his sleepy-looking eyes suddenly opening very wide. 'What have you got to say about it?'

With an effort Larry dragged his gaze away from the thing on the step and eyed the questioner suspiciously.

'I think you ought to do the explaining,' he said. 'Who are you, and how did this man get here?'

'Man? What man?' asked Margaret.

'There's been an accident, or something,' muttered Larry, and then, as the girl took a step forward: 'No, don't come any nearer. Stop her, Doctor, will you?'

Taplow moved forward, but she shook off his restraining hand and came over to the open door. As she saw the dead man she gave a little sobbing gasp and swayed. Larry thought she was going to faint, and his arm went out to catch her, but she recovered herself almost at once.

'How — how dreadful!' she said huskily. 'Is he dead?'

'I'm afraid so.' It was the slow voice of the big man that answered her. 'Do you know him, miss?'

She shook her head.

'Thought you might,' he went on, his half-closed eyes watching her. 'You seemed a bit upset when you saw him.'

'Wouldn't anyone be — ' began Larry, but the girl interrupted him.

'No, I don't know him,' she said. 'It was this, coming so soon after the other — '

She shuddered and stopped abruptly.

'The other?' The stout man stepped across the threshold. 'What do you mean?'

'Look here,' said Larry angrily, 'what right have you to ask all these questions?'

The other turned towards him, slowly nodded his large head, and began to unbutton his voluminous overcoat.

'That's a very natural question, sir,' he said with a smile, 'an' a very proper attitude to take up.' One of his huge hands fumbled in an inside pocket and produced a bulging wallet. From it he took a card. 'That's my right, sir,' he said, holding it out.

Larry took it, and read the inscription: 'Superintendent Robert Budd, C.I.D., New Scotland Yard, S.W.1.'

His eyebrows expressed his surprise.

'You're a — a detective!' he exclaimed in astonishment.

'Some people say so,' said Mr. Budd blandly. 'Others say I'm not. It seems to be a matter of opinion.' He turned his lazy eyes towards Margaret. 'Now, miss,' he went on, 'I'd like to know what you meant when you said 'so soon after the other'?'

'I — I meant Mr. Starl,' stammered the girl.

'Perhaps I'd better explain, Superintendent,' cut in Larry, coming to her rescue. 'Miss Lane has had rather a bad shock.'

'As long as somebody explains,' said the big man, 'it's O.K. with me.'

He listened with a rather bored expression while Larry told him as succinctly as possible what had happened.

'H'm!' he commented, suppressing a

yawn when the young lawyer had finished. 'Two dead men — one stabbed and the other strangled. A ladder against a window and the telephone put out of order.' He pursed his lips and scratched the side of his face with a large and thoughtful finger, 'All very perplexin' an' peculiar.'

'The telephone may only be a coincidence,' began Larry, but Mr. Budd shook his head.

'Those kinds of coincidences don't happen, Mr. Graham,' he said. 'I'd like to have a look round outside. Perhaps you, Doctor, will take a glance at this poor fellow while I do so.'

Taplow nodded.

'Certainly,' he said, and crossing to the open door, bent down and examined the man on the steps.

While he was so engaged, Mr. Budd borrowed Dillon's torch and, followed by Larry, went out into the rain. It was on the tip of the young lawyer's tongue to ask the detective why he had come to Moorland Lodge at all, but he concluded that this was not a propitious moment to put the question, and accordingly remained silent.

'Show me where this ladder is,' said the big Superintendent.

Larry led the way round the angle of the house until they came upon the ladder, still reared up against the wall.

Mr. Budd switched on the torch and carefully examined the ground. There was a confused jumble of footprints, but whether they conveyed anything to him, Larry could not fathom, for the detective made no comment.

Larry also saw that the surface of the path was churned up, and from the confusion ran two scored parallel lines.

'This is where the murder was committed,' grunted the big man. 'He was strangled here and dragged round and put on the steps. Those are the marks his heels made.'

He followed the tracks, and presently they found themselves back at the front door.

Dr. Taplow had completed his examination and was waiting for them.

Together Larry and Budd lifted the

dead man. He was unexpectedly light and, carrying him into the hall, they laid him, at Dillon's suggestion, on a settee in a small smoking room. Larry turned away as quickly as possible from the sight of that bloated face, but Mr. Budd was less squeamish. He stood looking down at the dead man and slowly shook his head.

'Poor old Joe,' he said presently, and catching the words, Larry swung round.

'Do you know him?' he asked quickly.

'Yes, I know him,' said Mr. Budd. 'Or, rather, I did know him. Joe Altman, one of the cleverest jewel thieves in the country. I pinched him four years ago, and got him five years. Allowing for remission of sentence for good conduct, he can't have been out so very long.'

'What brought him here?' demanded Larry.

'I don't know, Mr. Graham,' replied the big man slowly, 'but whatever he was after he got something that he didn't expect!'

5

The face at the window

In spite of the double tragedy that had taken place at Moorland Lodge that night, dinner was served as usual. It was a gloomy meal. Margaret Lane kept her eyes on her plate, eating scarcely anything, Mr. Budd was preoccupied and thoughtful, and although Larry tried once or twice to start a topic of conversation, he received no encouragement from the others.

Dr. Taplow had taken his departure almost immediately after his examination of the unfortunate Altman, and he had evidently kept his promise to notify the police, for three-quarters of an hour after he had gone an Inspector and two constables arrived.

In company with Superintendent Budd, they made an examination of the room upstairs and the exterior of the house, discovering nothing beyond the reason for the failure of the telephone to function. By the porch, where the wires passed into the open, a section, over a foot long, had been neatly removed. The Inspector, a brawny Yorkshireman, asked a number of questions, noted down the names of all the inmates of the house at the time of the murders, and took his departure, leaving one of the constables on guard.

Mr. Budd had been making inquiries concerning the nearest hotel when Margaret had put forward her suggestion that he should stay the night, a suggestion that he had accepted with surprising alacrity.

'Where shall I serve coffee, miss?' asked Dillon. 'In here, or in the drawing room?'

'I'll have mine in my room,' said Margaret quickly. 'Mr. Graham and the Superintendent will have theirs in the drawing room.'

As the butler bowed and withdrew, the girl rose to her feet.

'You'll excuse me, won't you,' she said, looking from one to the other. 'I — I have one or two things to do. I shall be upstairs if you want me.'

Larry opened the door for her, and she gave him a faint smile as she passed out.

Coming back to the table, Larry found Mr. Budd in the act of lighting a long, black cigar.

'Now,' he said, 'I'm going to ask you a question that I've been wanting to ask ever since you arrived.'

The stout man leaned back in his chair, which creaked ominously under his weight, and blew a stream of pungent-smelling smoke from between his lips.

'You want to know,' he said in his slow, ponderous way, 'what I came for?'

Larry smiled.

'Exactly,' he answered.

'Well,' said Mr. Budd, examining the end of his cigar through half-closed eyes. 'I came to see Mr. Starl.'

'I know that,' said Larry impatiently. 'But why did you come to see him? Did he send for you?'

The other's large head moved slowly from side to side.

'No, he didn't send for me,' he replied. 'I don't suppose he even knew I existed. I can understand you being curious, Mr.

Graham, but I'm afraid I can't satisfy your curiosity.'

'Well, tell me this,' said Larry. 'Has the reason for you being here got anything to do with these murders?'

'That I don't know,' answered Mr. Budd, 'an' I'm tellin' you the truth. Maybe it has — I should think very probably it has — but I can't see how at the moment. There are a lot of things that puzzle me, and one of them is the presence of that poor feller Altman.'

'Perhaps he killed Starl,' suggested Larry.

'He certainly climbed that ladder,' said the Superintendent. 'There was a shred of cloth attached to a nail near the top which corresponds with a tear in his coat, but I don't think he killed the old man. Joe wasn't a killer and, anyway, he certainly didn't kill himself. What puzzles me is why anyone should want to kill a man who was halfway dead already. Dr. Taplow says it was doubtful if Starl would have lived till the mornin'.'

'That struck me as curious,' said Larry. 'It's curious, too, that when the doctor went out the first time he saw nothing of Altman.'

'Not so curious if he was dead,' remarked the big Superintendent, expelling a huge cloud of smoke, and watching it drift towards the ceiling.

'The place where Altman was killed isn't visible from the spot where the doctor left his car and obviously his body wasn't put on the steps until Miss Lane had recalled Taplow to look at Starl.'

Suddenly, and with remarkable swiftness for a man of his bulk, he rose to his feet, crossed silently to the door, and jerked it open. Dillon, who was half-kneeling on the mat outside, almost fell into the room.

'Been there long?' asked Mr. Budd pleasantly.

Without a trace of embarrassment the butler shook his head.

'No, sir,' he answered, in his strange, whispering voice. 'I was just coming to tell you that your coffee is waiting in the drawing room.'

'I see.' The big man nodded and smiled slowly.

'And were you comin' into the room on all fours just to amuse us?'

'I noticed that my shoelace was untied,' explained Dillon, 'and I was stooping to re-tie it when you opened the door.' It was a lame explanation, and it convinced neither of his hearers. There was no doubt that Dillon had been listening. Mr. Budd said nothing, however, and suggested that they should go into the drawing room. When they were seated in front of the fire, and Dillon had served the coffee and gone, Larry looked across to his companion.

'Peculiar chap, isn't he?' grunted Budd placidly. 'Not the sort of feller I'd like around as a butler. That funny voice of his'd get on my nerves.' He yawned. 'You've asked me a lot of questions, Mr. Graham,' he went on. 'Now I'm goin' to ask you one. Why did Mr. Starl send for you so urgently?'

'I can only answer that the same as you answered me,' said Larry. 'I don't know.'

'He'd made a will, I suppose?' asked the other, and Larry nodded.

'Yes, several years ago,' he answered.

'Perhaps he was goin' to alter it?' suggested the Superintendent.

'That may have been his object,' assented Larry doubtfully, 'though there was no reason why he should. He had no kith or kin.'

'Who gets his money, then?' asked the big man.

'The British Museum,' replied Larry. 'Together with his Chinese collection.'

'I should like to see that,' said Mr. Budd surprisingly. 'Where does he keep it?'

'The collection?' asked Larry. 'In a big room, which they call the Museum.'

The stout Superintendent was interested.

'I wonder if we can have a look at it,' he said.

'I don't see why not.' Larry got up and rang the bell, and after a few seconds Dillon came in. 'We should like to have a look at Mr. Stall's collection, Dillon. Will you take us to the Museum?'

For a moment a startled expression appeared on the butler's face. It was gone in an instant, but Larry had both seen and noted it.

'I can take you to the room, sir,' said

Dillon, 'but you can't get in. At least, not without the keys.'

'Well, get them,' said Larry impatiently.

'I can't, sir,' answered the butler. 'They're with Mt. Starl. He kept them on a gold chain round his neck.'

'Well, they're easily got,' grunted Mr. Budd, rising to his feet. 'You show Mr. Graham the door of the room and I'll get the keys.'

He walked out into the hall and began laboriously to climb the staircase, while Dillon led Larry to the little room that Margaret Lane used as an office. Arrived there, Dillon pointed to the door set in the wall facing them.

'That's the entrance to the Museum, sir,' he said.

Larry went over and examined it. To his surprise he discovered that it was made of solid steel. Dillon noted his surprise.

'Yes, sir,' he said, 'it's like the door of a safe. I've seen it open once, and it's nearly six inches thick.'

'It seems an unusual precaution,' remarked the young lawyer.

'Mr. Starl was rather eccentric, sir,'

answered Dillon, 'but I expect you know that. This is the only means of getting into the Museum. There are no windows.'

Just then the sound of Mr. Budd's heavy steps descending the stairs reached them. A moment later the big man came in.

'There's the chain,' he said, dropping a fine gold chain on to the desk, 'but there are no keys. Somebody's taken 'em!'

Larry looked down at the chain, which Mr. Budd had dropped on the blotting-pad. A certain amount of violence had been used in taking the keys, for the small gold links were badly wrenched.

'Yes, they were torn away in a hurry,' said Budd, noting Larry examining the links. 'The chain had slipped down between his pyjama jacket and his back. That's why we didn't notice it before.'

Larry pursed his lips.

'Do you think that it was to get possession of the keys that he was killed?' he asked.

'It certainly looks like it,' answered the Superintendent. 'Obviously they were taken by the murderer.' He turned to

Dillon. The butler was looking at the chain with a queer expression in his eyes. 'I suppose,' said the detective, 'that those were the only keys to the Museum? Mr. Starl didn't keep a duplicate set?'

The butler shook his head.

'I don't think so, sir,' he replied, and his whisper was more pronounced than usual, as though a sudden dryness of his throat had added to his infirmity. 'Miss Lane can tell you more about that than I can.'

They sent for Margaret, and she came, her face anxious and troubled.

'No, there are no other keys,' she said, when Mr. Budd had put his question. 'Mr. Starl was most particular about nobody being able to enter the Museum unless he specially invited them. It took both keys to open the door, and when it's shut the room is practically a huge safe. I suppose the precaution was necessary. His collection is very valuable.'

'Have you ever been in the room?' asked the Superintendent, and she smiled.

'Oh, yes, several times!' she answered.

''But only when Mr. Starl was there himself.'

Mr. Budd nodded, his brows drawn together over his half-closed eyes.

'What does this collection consist of?' he asked presently.

'It's almost entirely Chinese,' replied Margaret. 'Mr. Starl was an authority on China and its history. He had collected some wonderful things, many of them the only specimens in existence and practically priceless.'

The stout man nodded again, his eyes thoughtfully surveying the broken chain.

'Did he go in at all for phil — what's the word — it means stamp collectin'?' he asked slowly.

'You mean philately?' said the girl, and shook her head. 'Not in the accepted sense. He has several rare Chinese stamps, but no others.'

'I see.' The big Superintendent's expression belied his words. 'I suppose you can't remember, Mr. Graham, whether this chain was round his neck when you found him?'

'No,' said Larry, 'but I don't see how it

45

could have been if the keys were taken by the murderer.'

'No, I suppose it couldn't, now you come to mention it,' said the other, as though this aspect hadn't struck him before. 'Well, well, it's very puzzlin'.' He suppressed a yawn. 'What do you make of it, Mr. Graham?'

'It looks to me as if robbery was the motive for the crime,' replied Larry, 'and that seems borne out by the presence of this man Altman. You say he was a burglar.'

'Not a burglar, Mr. Graham!' protested the big man, and the tone of his voice was almost shocked. 'Joe was an artist. His speciality was jewellery; he wouldn't have been interested in this Chinese stuff. No 'fence' would touch it. Besides, Altman was killed, too.'

'Well, it's pretty certain that somebody wanted those keys, and they could only have wanted them to get into the Museum,' said Larry, 'so robbery must be at the bottom of it.'

Mr. Budd nodded several times and gently massaged his lower lip.

'That sounds logical,' he admitted. 'Yes, I shouldn't be surprised if you weren't very nearly right, Mr. Graham — '

He broke off as Margaret uttered a startled cry. Her face had gone suddenly white and she was staring with wide eyes at something behind them. Both Larry and the big man swung round.,

There was a long, narrow window set in the wall at the back of them, and as they turned Larry caught a fleeting glimpse of a face pressed against the glass outside. It was only for an instant that he saw it, a smudged white oval. Then it was gone.

'Did you see it?' gasped the girl, her hand at her throat. 'A man's face looking in.'

'I saw something — ' began Larry, and stopped as the lethargic Mr. Budd became suddenly galvanised into action.

His huge bulk flashed past Larry, and he was outside the little room before they had quite realized what had happened. They heard him bark an order to the constable in the hall as he passed him on his way to the front door. By the time Larry reached the hall, Budd had jerked open the front door and disappeared in the darkness outside.

Larry caught up with the astonished constable at the foot of the steps, but already the big man was out of sight. They could hear his heavy footfalls going down the drive by the time they reached the front door, and there they stopped and listened, while Mr. Budd's retreating footsteps faded into silence. Then only the hissing of the rain and the dripping from the sodden bushes came to their ears.

A faint sound from behind them made Larry glance quickly over his shoulder, and he saw that Dillon had joined them.

'Did the man get away, sir?' whispered the butler excitedly.

'I don't know,' answered Larry a little shortly.

He was feeling in no mood to answer questions.

The constable suddenly gave an exclamation and pointed to a star-point of light that had flashed out of the darkness ahead.

'There's the Super, I think, sir,' he said. 'I'd better see if he wants me. Will you stay here, sir, and look after the house?'

He hurried away down the drive and became lost to sight. Larry waited impatiently, peering into the night.

Presently the light at the end of the drive grew brighter, and then Mr. Budd came back wearily, breathing hard and wiping his face.

'I saw him,' he said, 'but he had too big a start. He was down the drive and out the gate before I could catch up with him. But I know who he is, so it's not so bad as it might be.'

Larry, who had been unprepared for this, stopped and stared at the big man in astonishment.

'Who was he?' he demanded.

'I might almost call him an old friend,' replied the Superintendent, wiping the rain from his face and neck. 'I've got him many a 'stretch' in my time. Certainly he was a great friend of poor Joe Altman's. They were as thick as thieves, which is a pretty good simile when you come to think of it, for Luke Kelland is a thief if ever there was one.'

'Is that his name?' asked Larry,

'That's his name,' said Mr. Budd carefully. 'He has others. I don't think I've ever known a man with so many names, but Luke Kelland is the one we know him best by!'

6

The man in the garden

The household retired early. Margaret Lane, who looked tired and worn out, was the first to go, and Mr. Budd followed soon after. The soft-footed Dillon showed Larry to his room and, after inquiring if he wanted anything further, wished him good night and went about his business of locking up.

Larry's room was not as big as Benjamin Starl's bedroom, but it was very comfortable. A fire had been lighted in the grate and its red glow was very pleasant.

The rain was still falling heavily, and the wind had freshened, moaning round the house in intermittent gusts and blowing the drops against the windows with a sound like the side-drums in an orchestra. But Larry was tired out, and even the noise of the storm and the excitement of the day could not prevent him falling swiftly into a deep sleep.

Normally he was a light sleeper, and possessed the peculiar faculty of realizing what was happening before he was properly awake. Although still asleep, he knew that his door had opened and somebody had come into the room. He felt a hand touch his shoulder, and the intruder shook him gently. Instantly he was wide awake and sitting up in bed.

'I'm so sorry,' said the soft voice of Margaret Lane a little breathlessly, 'but I'm afraid. There's somebody in the grounds. Outside my window.'

Larry was out of bed in an instant. Pulling on his dressing gown, he went to the window and looked out.

It was still raining, but the wind had dropped, and the cold light of morning was in the sky. His window overlooked the back of the house, but there was nobody in sight.

'I couldn't sleep,' whispered Margaret, her voice trembling, 'and I was looking out of the window when I saw him. He was walking on the grass.'

'Who is it?' he asked.

She shook her head.

'I don't know. It was too dark to see,' she answered.

'I wonder if it is any good going after him,' muttered Larry, but she seemed reluctant to be left alone. And then:

'Look!' she breathed. 'Look!'

He caught his breath sharply as he saw what had attracted her attention. A figure had appeared, moving erratically towards the house. It was a man, and he was swaying from side to side as though drunk. As he staggered forward, his hand to his head, Larry pulled his arm away from the girl's fingers, and, hurrying out of the room, went racing down the stairs. He pulled back the bolts and the chain of the front door and, opening it, ran out into the open.

Hurrying round the side of the house, he saw the man again, moving unsteadily towards the back entrance. Just as Larry caught up with him he stumbled, and, but for the young lawyer's supporting arm, would have fallen.

'He got me!' he muttered, and

collapsed into Larry's arms.

Through the mask of blood that covered his face, Larry recognized him. It was Dillon!

Light footsteps behind him made Larry whirl round, half-expecting an attack. But it was only Margaret, who had followed him out, and between them they succeeded in getting the butler into the house.

He was still dressed in the clothes he had been wearing on the previous night, and from his appearance Larry concluded that he had not been to bed.

Margaret hurried away and came back with a bowl of water and a towel. Together they bathed the wound. It was in an ugly-looking place, just above his left eye, but so far as Larry could see, was not dangerous, though the skin had been cut for two or three inches and it had bled a good deal. By the time a rough dressing had been applied Dillon opened his eyes.

He looked about dazedly for a moment and muttered something that Larry did not catch. When he was able to walk the young lawyer assisted him upstairs to his room and helped him onto the bed.

'Now,' he said, when the butler was as comfortable as possible, 'Let's hear all about it. Who hit you?'

Dillon moistened his dry lips.

'That fellow who was looking in the window last night, sir,' he whispered.

'Oh, he came back, did he?' said Larry.

'Yes, he came back, sir,' answered the whispering man. 'I thought he would, and I was watching for him.'

'You didn't go to bed?'

It was more a statement than a question, and Dillon gave a slight smile.

'No, sir, I didn't go to bed,' he admitted. 'I wasn't very tired. I don't sleep very much at the best of times, and I thought it likely that this fellow would come back, so I determined to watch for him. It was beginning to get light when I saw him prowling about the house, and while he was round at the front I slipped out the back. My idea was to wait for him in the drive and catch him that way. As it was, he caught me.' He touched the bandage round his head with a little grimace of pain. 'I don't know what he hit me with, but it was something particularly hard.'

Larry eyed the man curiously. The story sounded plausible enough, except that it was hardly likely that an ordinary butler would have stopped up all night on the off-chance of a nocturnal prowler returning to take stock of the house. All along he had felt there was something peculiar about Dillon, and this last episode had strengthened this feeling.

'Look here, Dillon,' he said suddenly. 'What are you doing here? What do you know about this business?'

The butler's surprised expression was perfectly assumed if it was not genuine.

'I know nothing about it at all, sir,' he declared.

'I find that rather hard to believe,' retorted Larry,

'I'm sorry, sir, but it's the truth,' replied Dillon. 'Why should you think I know anything about it?'

The young lawyer shrugged his shoulders.

'Your whole manner,' he answered. 'I've been watching you, and I've noticed several peculiar things. For instance, when you brought that electric torch back just before the dead man was discovered on the steps, your coat was wet. You'd been out in the rain!'

'That's quite true, sir,' said the butler. 'One of the maids had been using the torch to fetch something from the outhouse and had left it there.'

'And then,' went on Larry, taking no notice of the explanation, 'you were listening at the door when Superintendent Budd and I were talking last night.'

'Perhaps I was, sir,' admitted Dillon, 'but there's nothing very much in that, is there? Two murders had been committed, and I was naturally rather curious.'

'Good butlers, as a rule, don't do that sort of thing,' remarked Larry.

'Perhaps I'm not a good butler, sir,' said Dillon and rather ostentatiously turned over on his side and closed his eyes.

Larry went back to his bedroom and dressed. When he came downstairs he found that Margaret had done the same. The servants were up by now and a fire had been lighted in the drawing room. A sleepy-eyed and startled maid brought them hot coffee, and they discussed the latest addition to the disturbing events at Moorland Lodge.

'What do you think can be at the bottom of it?' asked Margaret, setting down her empty cup and accepting a cigarette from Larry.

He shook his head.

'I don't know,' he answered. 'But I think your butler is mixed up in it somehow.'

'Dillon?'

She looked surprised.

'Yes. I'm pretty sure he knows more than he's said.'

'I don't like the man.' She frowned. 'I think I told you that, but I don't see why he should have had anything to do with Mr. Starl's murder.'

'I don't see why,' said Larry, 'but I'm certain he has.'

'What makes you think so?' she asked.

He told her. Put into words, his reasons seemed rather lame, and yet, in his own mind, he vas convinced that Dillon was by no means as ignorant as he made out.

'Have you mentioned this to Mr. Budd?' said Margaret. 'I think you should.'

'Should what?' remarked a sleepy voice at the door.

Mr. Budd, his round face beaming benevolently, came slowly into the room.

'If you didn't sleep so heavily,' said Larry, 'you'd know that things have been happening.'

The stout man crossed over to the fire and warmed his hands.

'Have I been neglectin' me duty?' he asked, shaking his head sadly. ''Don't tell me that that feller Kelland came back and injured poor Dillon.'

'You know?' exclaimed Larry. 'How?'

'Because I saw it happen,' said the superintendent slowly. 'Butlers are not the only people who stay awake all night, you know, Mr. Graham. It's quite a common habit in the police force.'

'If you saw it happen, why didn't you interfere?' asked the young lawyer.

'Because I didn't want to,' replied Mr. Budd, taking the cup of coffee that the girl had poured out. 'I was followin' a policy of masterly inactivity.' He took a sip of coffee and smacked his lips. 'I wish that manservant of yours hadn't been so conscientious,' he went on. 'He scared my bird off, which was a pity, because I was waitin' for him to lay his egg.'

'Perhaps you'll translate that into plain English,' said Larry irritably.

'Let me be mysterious, Mr. Graham,' pleaded the fat Superintendent, finishing his coffee at a gulp and setting down the empty cup. 'All detectives like to be mysterious, don't they, miss? As a matter of fact, I've been searchin' Dillon's room.'

'Searching Dillon's room?' cried the startled Larry. 'Is that what you did?'

'That's what I did, Mr. Graham,' nodded the big man.

'And did you find anything?' asked the girl.

Mr. Budd looked from one to the other as though he were peering over the tops of invisible glasses, a habit of his when he was particularly pleased with himself.

'Yes, I found somethin',' he replied complacently and, plunging his large hand into his pocket, he withdrew it and held it out for their inspection, palm upwards.

'Take a look at those.'

They looked and were thunderstruck.

'The missing keys!' Larry exclaimed,

7

The broken thread

Margaret drew in her breath sharply, and her face went white.

'You found them in Dillon's room?' she said in a horrified whisper.

Again Mr. Budd nodded.

'Yes,' he said, eyeing the keys with satisfaction. 'At the bottom of a vase on the mantelpiece.'

'Then Dillon must have killed Mr. Starl,' said the girl in a low voice.

'It doesn't necessarily follow that because he took the keys he killed the old gentleman,' remarked the detective.

'I don't think there's much doubt,' put in Larry. 'I thought there was something queer about that fellow the moment I saw him, and he had the opportunity. You remember he passed us in the corridor just before we made the discovery?'

Margaret nodded. Her troubled face

was puckered into a frown.

'But why did he do it?' she asked.

'We don't even know that he did do it,' said Mr. Budd. 'All we know is that he took the keys. We can't say that Mr. Starl wasn't dead when he took 'em.' He pinched a large fold of flesh below his chin and pursed his lips. 'It's all very puzzlin' an' peculiar, but I'd like to ask one thing. I don't want you to mention anythin' about my havin' found these keys. I'd rather only the three of us knew about that at the moment.'

He slipped them back in his pocket as he finished speaking.

'But surely Dillon will miss them — ' began Larry, and the Superintendent interrupted him.

'Maybe he will, maybe he won't,' he said. 'But, anyway, he won't know who's got 'em.'

A maid came at that moment to announce that breakfast was ready, and they went into the dining room. Larry discovered that early rising was conducive to hunger, and both he and Budd did full justice to the crisp, grilled bacon and kidneys that had been provided for them.

Margaret, however, ate little, contenting herself with a slice of toast.

Halfway through the meal Larry remembered something that he had intended asking the fat man before.

'What happened to that policeman who was here last night?' he said. 'Did he go back?'

Mr. Budd paused in the act of buttering a piece of toast and looked across at him queerly.

'No, he didn't go back, Mr. Graham,' he answered. 'He's still here.'

'Where?' demanded the young lawyer. 'I haven't seen anything of him.'

'You'd see him if you went into Miss Lane's office,' answered the other, reaching out a chubby hand for the marmalade. 'He's still asleep in the armchair.'

Larry laughed. It struck him as ludicrous that the man who had been left on guard should have slept while so many people had been up in that wakeful house. He said as much, but Mr. Budd shook his head.

'There's nothin' funny about it,' he said. 'Sleepin' caused by a dose of bromide ain't very funny.'

Larry stared aghast.

'Bromide?' he repeated incredulously. 'D'you mean the constable was drugged?'

The Superintendent swallowed a mouthful of toast and marmalade before he replied.

'That's exactly what I mean, Mr. Graham,' he said slowly. 'Somebody wanted him out of the way durin' the night, so they could have a free run.'

'Dillon,' murmured Margaret, and Mr. Budd gave her a quick glance.

'Yes, I think it was Dillon,' he said. 'In fact, I'm sure it was, because I found the bottle in his room from which the drug had been taken.'

'That means he did kill Starl,' declared Larry, 'and probably that fellow Altman as well. He'd been out just before you found the body.'

He told the interested detective of the rain on the butler's clothes, and of Dillon's plausible explanation. At this Budd frowned.

'I wish you hadn't let him know you suspected him, Mr. Graham,' he admonished gently. 'I really wish you hadn't.'

'What does it matter?' said Larry. 'You've got enough evidence to arrest him on suspicion.'

'Maybe I have,' replied Mr. Budd, 'but I'm not goin' to — not yet, at any rate.'

'Why do you think he drugged the constable?' asked Margaret. 'What did he want to do during the night?'

The stout Superintendent wiped his lips carefully, replaced his handkerchief in his pocket, and leaned back in his chair.

'That's fairly obvious, miss, isn't it?' he replied. 'He wanted an opportunity of enterin' the Museum.'

'I wonder if he succeeded?' said Larry.

'Somebody did,' answered the big man. 'I put a thread across the door last night, and when I looked this mornin' it was broken!'

★   ★   ★

Later on that morning the burly Yorkshire Inspector returned, and with him came the Chief Constable for the district. Mr. Budd had a long conference with the pair of them, and during this Larry wandered out into the grounds.

It was a grey day with a cold wind, but the rain had ceased, and although the ground was still wet and sloppy underfoot the air was refreshing.

He had many things to think about. Although, in his own mind, he was convinced that Dillon was at the bottom of the whole business, he couldn't see how Altman and the other man came into it. If they were working in league with the butler, why had one of them been killed? He had a feeling that Budd was keeping something back; that that sleepy-eyed, lethargic man knew a great deal more than he had divulged. The reason for his sudden appearance had yet to be explained.

His thoughts turned to Margaret Lane. Larry had met many women during his life, a great number of them beautiful, but none of them had succeeded in making such an impression as had this soft-voiced girl, with the pale face and big, questioning eyes. It came to him with something of a shock that the death of Starl would throw her out of employment, and he made a mental note to look into this and see if he could do anything to fix her up.

When he got back to the house, Larry found that the conference between the three police officials had finished. Mr. Budd came to him and drew him to one side.

'I'm goin' over to Lastingham,' he said. 'I've got one or two inquiries I'd like to make. Perhaps, Mr. Graham, you'd like to come with me?'

Larry agreed, for this fitted in with his own plans.

The Inspector and the Chief Constable took their departure, and with them went the yawning and still sleepy policeman. His relief had come over with the Inspector, a stolid, red-faced man, who took up his position in Margaret Lane's little office and looked as though nothing short of an earthquake would shift him.

Mr. Budd was silent while Larry drove him to Lastingham, and so evidently preoccupied with his thoughts that Larry refrained from interrupting him.

They stopped first at the small post

office, and the young lawyer put through a call to London, spoke to Mr. Carlock, and presently rejoined the stout Superintendent.

'Now I've done all I want to do,' he said. 'Where can I take you?'

'I think we'll go and see what the Yorkshire beer's like,' remarked Budd. 'I've heard it's very good in these parts.'

Larry looked about him. A few yards up the street was a small public house. Mr. Budd eyed it and shook his head disapprovingly.

'Doesn't seem to me the sort of place where they'd sell the right kind of beer,' he said. 'The Inspector tells me there's a place called the Crown where the beer is really beer. Suppose we try that?'

The Crown, on the fringe of the village, was a much more pretentious place than Larry had expected. Originally it had probably been an old post-house, for the main road ran past its entrance. He stopped the car, and Budd got heavily out.

The saloon bar was practically empty. Two men, who looked like farmers, were talking in low tones, and a small, dapper man was gloomily drinking a double whisky by himself.

The dapper little man looked round as they approached the bar, and as he caught sight of the huge figure of Mr. Budd he gave a violent start and almost dropped the glass he was holding.

The stout Superintendent stopped, and his face was the picture of innocent surprise.

'Dear me,' he said, 'now isn't the world a small place? Who'd have thought of meetin' you in Yorkshire?'

The dapper man eyed him coldly.

'I think you've made a mistake,' he began, but Budd interrupted him.

'I couldn't make a mistake with such an old friend as you,' he said reproachfully. 'Meet my friend Mr. Graham, Kelland, and tell us what you're doin' in this part of the world.'

8

Kelland's story

Larry started. So this small, neatly-dressed man was Luke Kelland, friend and partner of Joe Altman, and the man who had been lurking about in the vicinity of Moorland Lodge! This was the reason for Budd's sudden desire to sample the beer offered by the Crown, though how he knew where he would find the man was a mystery beyond Larry's capacity to fathom.

'I don't know what you're talking about,' said Kelland surlily. 'You've made a mistake. My name isn't Kelland. It's Lester.'

'Dear me,' said Mr. Budd, shaking his head sadly. 'How do you find all these names? Whenever I meet you you've got a different one. Lester now, is it? Well, well.'

The man gulped down his whisky and turned his eyes towards Larry. Unpleasant eyes, they were, of the palest shade of blue.

'Is your friend mad?' he asked. 'Is he in the habit of mistaking perfect strangers for friends of his?'

'Not perfect,' said Budd, shaking his head before Larry had time to reply. 'Nobody could call you perfect, Luke. How's your pal Joe?'

The man's eyes snapped angrily.

'I don't know anybody called Joe,' he said harshly.

'Dear me, has he changed his name, too?' asked the fat detective, with an expression of well-simulated surprise. 'How you fellers do ring the changes!'

Kelland looked at him, his thin face a shade paler.

'I don't know what you mean,' he muttered. 'You've got nothing on me, even if I am Kelland. I'm turning straight now.'

'You weren't when I was chasin' you last night,' interrupted Mr. Budd, his expression relapsing into its habitual good humour. 'I've never seen a feller run so erratically. What were you doin' at Moorland Lodge?'

Luke Kelland licked his thin lips.

'I was looking for Altman,' he said reluctantly.

Mr. Budd took a long pull at his tankard and nodded slowly.

'You were lookin' for Joe, eh? Why did you expect to find Joe there?'

Mr. Kelland assumed an expression of great candour.

'The truth of the matter, Superintendent,' he said, 'is that Joe had a confidential business appointment with Mr. Starl, and before he went he said he'd come back and pick me up here. Well, when he didn't return, I got a bit anxious and went to look for him.'

'Afraid he was goin' to double-cross you,' murmured the stout man. 'Go on!'

'That's all,' said Kelland with an expressive gesture. 'When I saw I'd been spotted looking in the window I did a runner.'

'An' came back in the small hours of the mornin' to have another look?' suggested Mr. Budd.

'Well, yes, I did,' said the other, rather taken aback.

'Did you know that Benjamin Starl was

murdered in his bed yesterday evenin'?' asked the Superintendent suddenly.

The glass that Kelland was raising to his lips fell from his nerveless fingers and smashed on the floor. His face went a dirty grey, and he stared at Mr. Budd with dropped jaw.

'Murdered?' he almost squeaked. 'Yesterday evening? I knew nothing about it. You're not trying to put it on me, are you?'

There was real terror in the pale eyes.

'I'm not tryin' to put it on anybody — yet!' said the Superintendent. 'I'm just gatherin' information.'

'It must have been Altman who did it,' muttered Kelland, wiping the perspiration from his forehead. 'That's why he never came back.'

'He may have killed Starl, but that isn't the reason he didn't come back,' said Mr. Budd. 'He didn't come back because he couldn't come back.'

'D'you mean he was pinched?' asked Kelland.

'No, I mean he was killed,' answered the big man. 'Somebody strangled him!'

If Kelland had been shocked by the news of Starl's death, the murder of his friend was an infinitely greater blow.

'Joe — strangled?' he mumbled, when at last he could find words. 'But who — who could have done it?'

'You were in the vicinity,' pointed out the detective gently.

'Me?' exclaimed Kelland. 'Why should I have wanted to kill Joe? Why, he only came out of stir the day before yesterday.'

'Well, somebody killed him,' said the Superintendent, 'and somebody killed Starl. Whether you killed both or whether Altman killed Starl and then you killed Altman, I don't know.'

'I didn't kill neither of them,' insisted Kelland vehemently. 'Get that. I didn't know they were dead until you told me.'

Larry was inclined to believe the man. His surprise and distress were so obviously sincere. He looked at the stout Superintendent, but that worthy was staring with half-closed eyes into his tankard, and whatever his thoughts may have been there was no clue to them in his expression.

'What was this business?' he asked presently. 'What did Altman want with Starl?'

Kelland hesitated and, seeing his hesitation, the fat man went on.

'Perhaps you'd rather come along to the police station and tell the local Inspector?'

'No, I'll tell you,' said the other hastily. 'It started five years ago — before Joe got his stretch. Do you remember the robbery at the Royal Philatelic Museum?'

Mr. Budd started.

'So that's it, is it?' he said softly. 'Yes, I remember it, 'cause I was in charge of the case. This is very interestin'. Altman couldn't have had anythin' to do with that, because he was in America at the time.'

'He didn't,' said Kelland hastily. 'Neither had I, but Benjamin Starl wanted the Orange Triangle, and it was through me and Joe Altman that he got it!'

9

The Orange Triangle

Larry Graham's complete bewilderment was pictured on his face.

'What on earth is the Orange Triangle?' he asked.

Mr. Budd smiled.

'The Orange Triangle is a stamp,' he explained. 'About ten years ago the State of Hen-Yat in China decided to alter the design of their stamps. The new issue was on the point of bein' put on sale when the buildin' caught fire, and the whole shoot, with the exception of one stamp, was destroyed. This stamp, which was, naturally, of incalculable value, became the property of the Royal Philatelic Museum. Its estimated value was somethin' in the region of ten thousand pounds, but in the eyes of collectors it was priceless, bein' the only one of its kind in the world. It was kept in a sealed box in the Museum's strongroom, and was only exhibited to very privileged visitors. One night the place was burgled and the stamp was stolen. Since then all trace of it was lost, although we have had detectives workin' on the case. We had our suspicions that it had been smuggled out of the country.'

'I see,' said Larry, a light breaking on him. 'And that stamp is in the collection of Benjamin Starl.'

'That's right,' said Mr. Budd. 'I've suspected it was there for a long time — that's what I came to see him about — now I'm sure.' He turned to Kelland. 'Finish your story.'

The little crook took a sip of his drink.

'There isn't much to tell,' he said. 'I get to hear a lot of things, one way and another, and soon after the robbery I heard that this stamp had gone to America. There was a very rich fellow over there whose hobby was stamp-collecting, and it had got round amongst the 'regulars' that he was prepared to offer a big sum for this Orange Triangle, and no questions asked.

'I know who did the Museum robbery

but I'm not telling you that, and I know how much he got for the stamp. It struck me as being money for jam at the time, but I thought no more about it until it came to my ears that there was a fellow in England who was prepared to pay five thousand pounds to have it pinched from this other chap. Joe was in America at the time, and I wrote over to him suggesting that he should do the job. He did it and came back to England with the stamp.' He explained the disasters that had happened to the unfortunate Mr. Altman. 'I was in fifty-fifty with him and, naturally, when he came out of 'boob', I met him, and we came up here to collect the five thousand the old gentleman had promised. Joe rang him up from this very place, and was told that he was ill, He thought it was an excuse to get out of paying him for his money, and went up to Moorland Lodge to try and get an interview with Starl. That's the last I saw of him, and until you blew in here this morning I thought he'd done the dirty on me.'

'Now we know why the keys were stolen,'

remarked Larry, looking across at Budd, when Kelland had finished speaking.

The fat man nodded.

'Yes, we know quite a bit now,' he answered, 'but we don't know it all.'

'You know all I know,' declared Kelland quickly.

The detective made no reply, but, finishing his tankard of beer, rose ponderously to his feet.

'I'm afraid I shall have to ask you to come with me to the station,' he said.

The dapper little man looked at him in alarm.

'Here, what's the idea?' he exclaimed. 'You're not pinching me, are you?'

The detective shook his head.

'I'm only detainin' you as an important witness at present,' he answered. 'I can't afford to run the risk of you clearin' out, so you'd better pay your bill here and come with me.'

Kelland was inclined to be argumentative, but the Superintendent overruled his arguments and accompanied him to the manager.

'How did you know he was staying here?' asked Larry curiously, while

Kelland was settling his bill.

'I knew he was stayin' somewhere,' answered Mr. Budd wearily, 'and this is the only pub in the place that has accommodation for guests, so it wasn't very difficult.'

Larry expected that as soon as Kelland had been handed over to the care of the local police they would return to Moorland Lodge, but apparently Budd had no such intention, for when they came out of the little police station he paused hesitantly on the pavement and rubbed his massive chins.

'Now I've got one or two calls to make, Mr. Graham,' he said, 'and I don't think you'd be very interested. Apart from which, I don't want to keep you hangin' about, and I may be some time, so I'll see you back at the house.'

Larry was curious, and would infinitely have preferred to accompany the Superintendent wherever he might happen to be going. But Mr. Budd had suddenly conceived an urgent desire for his own company, and refused to listen to Larry's suggestion.

'No, I'll see you at Moorland Lodge

later on,' he repeated, and as the young lawyer climbed back into his car he began to move ponderously away up the narrow street.

Larry found Margaret in the drawing room when he got back, and learned from her that nothing had happened during their absence.

When he told her about the stamp, she evinced little surprise.

'Mr. Starl was capable of going to any lengths to obtain what he wanted for his collection,' she said, 'although, of course, he never told me anything about it. I suppose that's why, when he knew he was dying, he was so insistent on sending for Mr. Carlock.'

This had not struck Larry before, but it seemed to be a reasonable explanation for the old man's urgent message.

'I think you're right,' he said. 'Things seem to be explaining themselves rapidly.'

'We still don't know who killed Mr. Starl and the other man,' she said in a low voice.

Larry looked at her steadily.

'Don't we?' he said. 'I've a pretty good idea.'

'You mean Dillon?' she asked.

He nodded.

'Yes, I suppose so,' she said, and shivered. 'It's — it's horrible to know there's a murderer in the house. Not that I shall be here long,' she added.

Larry was quick to seize the opportunity she offered.

'What are you going to do?' he asked.

She shook her head.

'I don't know.'

'I may be able to help you,' said Larry, and the smile she gave him made his heart miss a beat.

'It's very kind of you, Mr. Graham,' she said gratefully. 'Though there's really no reason why you should trouble.'

'Isn't there?' said Larry a little huskily, and before either of them quite knew what had happened she was in his arms, and his lips were seeking hers.

When Mr. Budd came back at six o'clock that evening he found two radiant young people. He was momentarily puzzled to account for the cause until he happened to intercept a glance between them, and then he smiled to himself.

Dr. Taplow had driven him back, but the jovial-faced little man refused Margaret's invitation to stop to dinner.

'Afraid I can't, Miss Lane. There's an epidemic of influenza at Lastingham, and I've scarcely got a moment to breathe.'

He said goodbye and bustled off to his car.

When he had gone, Larry drew the big Superintendent aside.

'Don't you think,' he said, 'that you ought to arrest Dillon on suspicion? I'm pretty certain the man's guilty, and he may get away if you don't. We know he took those keys, and — '

Something in Mr. Budd's expression stopped him.

'Do we, Mr. Graham?' he said gently. 'I don't think we do. You see, those keys I found in his room aren't the keys at all.'

Larry was staggered.

'Do you mean they're not the keys of the Museum?' he asked incredulously.

'Oh, they're the keys of the Museum all right!' answered Mr. Budd, 'but they're not the keys that were stolen from the chain around Benjamin Stall's neck!'

10

Moving shadows

Larry stared at the smiling, complacent face of the fat detective, too astonished for the moment to put into words the questions that were on the tip of his tongue.

'How do you know this?' he managed to ask at length.

'It's very simple,' replied Mr. Budd. 'I had another look at those keys, and it struck me that they seemed rather new, so I examined the handle part. Now if they'd been constantly kept on that chain as they were supposed to have been, it would have worn a shiny place inside the top. There wasn't any such mark.'

'Then there are two sets of keys,' said Larry rather unnecessarily, and the superintendent suppressed a yawn.

'Obviously,' he remarked dryly. 'Let's go and have a word with Miss Lane.'

The girl was as much surprised as Larry had been.

'I don't know where they could have come from,' she said. 'I'm certain Mr. Starl only had the one set.'

'So am I,' murmured Mr. Budd, rubbing the side of his nose gently. 'Would Dillon have had any opportunity of gettin' an impression of the real keys?'

She began to shake her head, and then stopped abruptly.

'Why, yes, he would,' she said excitedly. 'I've just remembered. Mr. Starl had a heart attack about two weeks ago. He fainted one morning in his bedroom, and it was Dillon who found him.'

A pleased expression flitted across the big man's face.

'That's it,' he said. 'He must have taken an impression while the old gentleman was unconscious, and had the other keys made.'

Larry frowned.

'Well, if he already had a set of keys to the Museum, why did he kill Starl?' he demanded.

Mr. Budd sighed and shook his head sadly.

'It's all very complicated and mysterious,' he replied. 'Perhaps I'll be able to tell you more about it when I come back.'

'From where?' asked Larry.

The evening was providing him with a succession of surprises.

'From London,' was the unexpected answer. 'I'm leavin' in about ten minutes.'

Larry tried to discover the reason for this sudden departure, but the stout man was evasive. Nor would he listen to Margaret's entreaties that he should have dinner before he left.

'No, miss,' he said, 'business before pleasure is my motto. I'll stop for a bite on the way.'

It was a quarter-to-seven when he left, and as the sound of the car faded in the distance Margaret felt a twinge of uneasiness.

'I wish he'd waited till the morning,' she muttered with a shiver. 'I should have felt more comfortable if he'd been in the house tonight.'

★   ★   ★

Night came slowly down on the house and on the wild waste of moorland that surrounded it. Across the lowering sky woolly rain clouds scudded before the wind, and the gaunt trees tossed their branches, creaking and groaning at the disturber of their peace. One by one the lights in the lonely house went out until only a solitary glimmer shone from an upper window.

In this room Dillon sat on the edge of his narrow bed, his shaggy brows drawn together in a frown, reading for the twentieth time the note that had reached him that evening. Presently he got up and, lighting a cigarette, paced up and down the small chamber, his sallow face set in a thoughtful expression. It was past midnight, but he made no effort to undress. Several times he paused by the window, and drawing aside the curtain, peered out into the darkness.

He finished his cigarette, glanced at a small clock on the mantelpiece and, going to a cupboard in which he kept his clothes, took a thick coat and a hat. Putting them on, he picked up an electric hand-lamp, tested it, and, switching out the light, left his room, closing the door behind him.

The constable who had been left on guard had gone, in response to a message sent up by the Inspector at Lastingham.

A moving shadow in a house of shadows, Dillon crossed the hall, negotiated the short passage that led to the back of the premises, and paused at the back door. For a moment he hesitated, listening, and then stealthily pulled back the bolt and turned the key in the lock.

As he pulled the door open a cold gust of wind blew in, rustling a newspaper that had been left on the table behind him. The butler swung round, his nerves tense, and flashed on his light. Seeing what it was that had startled him he gave a sigh of relief. For the moment he had imagined that somebody had moved in the kitchen.

He slipped out through the back door and pulled it to after him.

Walking on the grass so that his footsteps were deadened, he made his way to a small group of trees near the entrance to the drive. As he reached them, a man came from the shelter of their trunks. Dillon stopped, and they conversed for several minutes, speaking in barely audible whispers — the butler rapidly, the other man interjecting a word here and there. Presently they began to move towards the house.

The first drops of the threatened rain began to fall as Dillon opened the door and entered with his companion. Without a sound the door was closed and locked, and they passed on into the silent darkness of the sleeping house.

11

Someone in the house

Margaret Lane, wakeful and restless, lay staring at the invisible ceiling of her bedroom. Twice she had put on the light and tried to read. Twice she had resolutely put it out again and made up her mind to sleep, but sleep eluded her.

Suddenly she sat bolt upright, her mouth and throat dry and her heart beating thunderously. From somewhere in the house a sound had reached her. She strained her ears, but it did not come again — that soft footfall which had startled her into a panic. Somebody was moving about in the hall below.

Margaret slipped out of bed, thrust her feet into slippers, and pulled on a dressing gown. Her teeth were chattering as she felt her way to the door. An unreasoning, almost paralyzing terror was gripping her. Not for a thousand pounds would she have stayed any longer by herself in that room. She must find and waken Larry. Only his presence could allay her fears.

The corridor was dark and cold, and her knees were shaking, but she found the door of his room and, turning the handle, entered. And here she got a shock, for, stooping over the bed to waken him, she found that it was empty. Larry was not there!

She stood in the darkness, breathing quickly, her hand at her throat. Perhaps it was his step she had heard.

Moving along to the head of the stairs, she reached out her hand for the banisters, and nearly screamed as it came in contact with warm flesh. The next second her terror was changed to relief, for it was Larry.

He was leaning over, peering into the dark well below. He pressed her arm as a warning not to speak, and together they looked down into the hall.

Suddenly a glimmer of light flashed fan-shaped across the hall below, and it came through the half-closed door of her office.

'I'm going to see who it is,' whispered Larry, and before she could stop him began to move stealthily down the staircase.

Margaret followed, curiosity overcoming her fear.

The light had vanished and all was dark again when they reached the hall, but from the office they heard the sound of metal against metal, followed by two barely audible clicks. There was no need to ask what the sound portended. Somebody had opened the safe-like door of the Museum.

On tiptoe Larry went across the big hall. Outside the office he paused, then, after a second's hesitation, pushed at the partly opened door and swung it another foot. Craning forward warily, he peered into the room. It was in darkness, and, so far as he could tell, empty, but the steel door of the Museum was a few inches ajar, and from inside a light filtered round the edge. Larry compressed his lips grimly.

Gingerly he left his position by the office door, and crossing the little room grasped the heavy door of the Museum by its edge and began to pull it gently farther open. He felt Margaret's quick breath on his cheek as the weighty mass of steel slowly moved, inch by inch.

After what seemed an age he was able to see into the long room beyond. A tiny spark of light — or so it appeared in that vast darkness — came from an electric hand-lamp that stood on the top of a glass case. Its light was directed on one of the walls, and silhouetted against that patch of radiance was the figure of a man. His back was towards the watchers, and he was bending forward, apparently doing something to one of the panels. In his excitement Larry took a step forward, and disaster overwhelmed him.

When he had first been aroused by movements in the house he had not waited to put on slippers, and his toe came in violent contact with the steel surround into which the door fitted. Before he could stop himself he had uttered a smothered cry.

The man by the wall swung round with an oath. Larry, through streaming eyes, caught a glimpse of a masked face — and then the light went out.

He heard a rush of feet and, with a flash of inspiration, slammed the heavy steel door to. It shut with a soft thud, and he heard the bolts clang into their sockets. Stumbling over to the switch, he pressed it down and flooded the office with light.

'Well, that settles our friend, whoever he is,' he gasped grimly, turning to the pale-faced girl.

'Who was it?' whispered Margaret.

'I — ' began Larry, and broke off.

From behind the closed steel door came the muffled sound of a shot. It was followed by another almost immediately, and then the rumbling mutter of voices.

'Good lord, there's more than one of them!' exclaimed Larry, aghast, and then he got his greatest shock of that night.

Somebody banged softly on the inside of the closed door.

'Open the door, will you, Mr. Graham,' came the faint but unmistakable voice of Mr. Budd. 'I'm not very interested in Chinese relics, but I've got somethin' here that I want to put in my criminal museum!'

When at last Larry recovered from his surprise at the sound of the Superintendent's voice, he stepped forward and twisted the keys of the double locks. The door opened slowly, and Mr. Budd emerged.

He was clad in a heavy overcoat, and wore a bowler hat on the back of his head. He blinked sleepily at Larry and the astonished girl.

'Thanks!' he said briefly, putting the automatic he had been holding in his pocket. 'Do you know how the lights work in here, Miss Lane?'

Margaret nodded.

'The switch is above the door,' she answered.

The detective thanked her, and, going inside the Museum, reached up an arm and fumbled for a moment over the steel door. There was a click and the big room became flooded with light.

'That's better,' murmured Mr. Budd.

He picked his way between the rows of glass cabinets to the spot in the wall, which had occupied the masked man's attention.

A section of the polished wood panelling was open, and in the aperture it had concealed, Larry, who had followed the Yard man, saw a small safe. The door of this was partly open, too, with the key that had unlocked it still in the lock. The detective groped about inside the safe and brought to light a small box of Chinese lacquer. Opening it, he peered at its contents, gave a little chuckle of satisfaction, and turned to Larry.

'The Orange Triangle!' he said complacently. 'You'd never think it was worth all that money, would you, to look at it?'

Larry looked at the small object resting under a glass frame, and agreed.

'The cause of two men's deaths,' remarked Mr. Budd, shaking his head, 'and it'll be the cause of another when the law's had its way.'

His eyes went past Larry to the other side of the room beside the door. Following the direction of his gaze, the young lawyer saw a sprawling figure, handcuffs on its wrists, lying prone and motionless on the floor.

'Afraid I had to hit him rather hard,' said the Superintendent apologetically, 'but I'm scared of firearms, and he shot twice.'

'Who is it?' asked Larry curiously.

'It's the man who stabbed Starl and strangled Altman,' answered Mr. Budd. 'A nasty feller, though you wouldn't think it to look at him.'

He walked over to the recumbent form and turned it over on to its back.

The unconscious man was Dr. Taplow!

12

The man from America

Mr. Budd gulped down the hot coffee that Margaret had poured out for him, smacked his lips in appreciation, and put the empty cup back on the table.

'Yes, it was Taplow,' he remarked. 'And we might never have been able to fix it on him if he hadn't walked into the trap I set.'

'How did you know it was the doctor?' asked Larry.

The Yard man smiled.

'I didn't for certain till tonight,' he confessed, 'but I suspected him from the first. He had a better opportunity than anybody. He was alone with Starl just before you discovered he had been killed. D'you remember what I said about jumpin' to conclusions? It was all this business of Altman's and Kelland's and Dillon's that distracted the

99

attention from Taplow.

'If Altman hadn't tried to get a private interview with Starl by climbin' that ladder; if Dillon hadn't got those extra keys cut, and if Kelland hadn't come back to look for his friend, Taplow's guilt would have stood out a mile.'

'Yes, I suppose you're right,' agreed Larry. 'Why did he strangle Altman?'

'Because he had to,' answered the Superintendent, yawning. 'Altman saw him stab Starl, and tackled him with the crime. Taplow had to kill him to save himself.'

'And was he after the stamp, Mr. Budd?' asked Margaret.

The detective nodded.

'Yes,' he replied. 'When I stayed behind in Lastingham yesterday I made several inquiries about Dr. Taplow. One thing I learned was that his hobby was stamp-collectin', and another that he was very hard up. He was owing money everywhere. He was a confirmed gambler, played the races, and dabbled on the Stock Exchange. I put a call through to London, and they knew all about him at the Yard. He hadn't got too good a reputation, and there were judgment summonses out all over the place.

'Starl's conscience began to trouble him when he found he was dying. He'd got this business of the stamp on his mind, an' he wanted to get it cleared up. He sent through to you, askin' you to come down to see him at once. Bein' afraid that he might peg out before you arrived, he made a confidant of Taplow. He told him all about the stamp, where it was hidden, and showed him the keys of the Museum.

'Bein' a collector, he knew the value of the Orange Triangle, and also knew that there were a good many other people in the world who would be willin' to buy it without askin' any questions. He stabbed Starl, secured the keys, and then got the shock of his life, for he saw Altman at the window watchin' him. We can pretty well guess what passed between them. Altman was a crook, and I suppose he tried to blackmail Taplow. Taplow arranged to meet him outside, and hurried downstairs, as you know. He went out, ostensibly on his way home, met Altman, and strangled him, puttin' the body on the steps.

'So far, everything was plain sailin'. All he had to do now was to wait an opportunity to secure the stamp. He had the keys, and he knew where it was. I gave him the opportunity tonight.

'I guessed that Taplow would take advantage of the fact and make a bid for the stamp. He did, and when he came I was waitin' for him in the Museum. I didn't want to pinch him until he'd shown me where the stamp was hidden.'

'How did you get into the Museum?' demanded Larry.

The fat man looked at him with a twinkle in his eye.

'I was let into the house by Dillon,' he replied. 'I sent him a note askin' him to meet me at one o'clock, tellin' him that if he didn't keep the appointment I'd arrest him.'

'I thought he was a crook,' said the young lawyer. 'I suppose he was also after the stamp?'

Mr. Budd nodded.

'He was after the stamp all right,' he replied, 'but he isn't a crook, he's a detective!'

His words supplied Larry with his crowning surprise.

'A detective?' he echoed. 'Do you mean a Scotland Yard man?'

The Superintendent shook his head.

'No,' he said. 'Dillon hails from America. He's a private detective. There are quite a lot of 'em out there, as you know, and he was engaged by the man from whom Altman stole the stamp in the first place. This feller, who is a millionaire, offered Dillon's firm a colossal sum to get the thing back. Dillon told me all this when I threatened him with arrest.'

'So that's why he had the keys cut.'

'That's why,' said Mr. Budd. 'He'd spent many nights searchin' the Museum tryin' to find the stamp's hidin' place, but without success.' He gave a prodigious yawn and looked at his watch. 'Well,' he said, 'I'd like to get a little sleep in before I return to London, and as it's nearly four, I think we'd better go to bed.' He rose ponderously to his feet and crossed to the door. 'Good night,' he said. 'Oh, and by the way! In the excitement I forgot to offer you my congratulations.'

Margaret reddened.

'How — how did you know?' she gasped.

Mr. Budd's large face creased into a smile.

'Just logical deduction,' he answered. 'When I see two young people givin' each other gooey glances, an' surprise 'em holdin' hands when they think nobody's lookin', I naturally put two and two together. Goodnight!'

2

THE BLACK WIDOW

1

Death in the fog

Mr. Budd opened his eyes as the crawling police car came to a stop and looked out at the blackness beyond the windows.

'Where are we now?' he grunted.

The driver twisted round in his seat and shook his head.

'I don't know, sir,' he confessed candidly.

'Must be somewhere between Tavistock and Princetown,' put in the melancholy voice of Sergeant Leek.

'You said that an hour ago,' remarked the stout Superintendent irritably. 'I know we're somewhere between Tavistock and Princetown, but where?'

The man at the wheel leaned forward and peered through the windscreen into the dense blanket of fog that closed them in and which the lights of the car only rendered more opaque.

'I can't see anything, sir,' he announced. 'I must have got off the main road somewhere. I don't know where we are, and that's a fact.'

'We must be somewhere on Dartmoor — ' began Leek intelligently.

'Of course we're on Dartmoor,' broke in Mr. Budd impatiently. 'Did you think this was the middle of the Sahara Desert or the great Alkali Plain?'

The thin sergeant sighed audibly. His superior was going to be difficult — he recognized the signs — and it was bad enough being stranded in that blinding mist without Mr. Budd's pleasantries to make the situation worse.

'I was only saying — ' he ventured in an injured voice, but again the stout man interrupted him.

'If you'd say less and think more you might be of some use!' he said scathingly. 'What are we goin' to do, Spencer?'

The police driver scratched his head, obviously at a loss.

'I'll go forward if you like, sir,' he replied without enthusiasm, 'but it's thicker here than ever.'

'What's the use of goin' forward if you don't know where you're goin'?' said Mr. Budd.

His question was unanswerable.

'Suppose we try goin' back to Tavistock?' suggested Leek, with visions of warm food and a comfortable fire.

'If we can't go on we can't go back,' said Mr. Budd. 'That's sense, though I don't expect you've ever heard of the word!'

'Well, we can't stop here,' protested the sergeant in dismay.

'We *have* stopped here,' grunted the Superintendent. 'What's the use of makin' stupid statements like that?'

'I mean,' explained the long-suffering Leek, 'that we can't go on stopping here — not all night.'

'Why not?' demanded Mr. Budd. 'I don't see what else we can do — unless you've got some bright idea for clearin' the fog away.'

'There's nothin' I can do,' said the sergeant.

'I've thought that for a long time,' said the stout man. 'I'm glad you've admitted it at last.'

The miserable Leek pulled his coat round him and subsided into his corner.

'Shall I go and have a look round, sir?' asked the driver.

Mr. Budd nodded ponderously.

'Maybe that 'ud be a good idea,' he said. 'If we're still on the main road we could go on then, even if it was only slowly.'

Detective Constable Spencer took an electric torch from the door pocket at his side, opened the door, and stepped out into the thick, white vapour, closing the door behind him. As he passed round in front of the standing car his shadow, grotesque and curiously unreal, was thrown by the headlights on to the wall of fog, and then both he and it disappeared, seeming to melt away like butter before a furnace.

For a moment or two they heard the sound of his uncertain steps then they, too, ceased and there was silence, that peculiar dead silence which is the special characteristic of a fog.

About them was an infinite loneliness. They might have been atoms in limitless space for the world seemed to have stopped. Mr. Budd closed his eyes and settled his huge bulk comfortably against the cushions.

They had left London that November morning in bright sunshine with the intention of reaching Princetown and the great convict prison by evening. Outside Tavistock they had run into the fog, one of those swift, impenetrable mists that rise suddenly and without warning on Dartmoor and blot out the entire landscape.

'Looks as if we shan't see Princetown tonight,' remarked Sergeant Leek gloomily.

Mr. Budd grunted.

'They'll be wondering what's happened to us,' went on the sergeant.

'I expect they will,' said the stout man. 'It'll never occur to 'em that we've been held up by the fog. They'll think we've been kidnapped by fairies or somethin' like that.'

He yawned wearily and Leek searched round for another subject of conversation.

'I wonder if we'll get anythin' out o' Wenham?' he said musingly.

111

'I doubt it,' answered Mr. Budd. 'We haven't been able to get anythin' out of him for five years, so I don't see why he should squeal now. Even if he's alive when we get there,' he added pessimistically.

'What's the matter with 'im?' asked Leek.

'Lobar pneumonia,' answered the stout Superintendent briefly. 'An' you don't stand much chance with that. He's only conscious for short periods.'

Charles Wenham was a thorn in Mr. Budd's side. It had been he who had arrested the man after the robbery at Mornington's, the wholesale jewellers, when Wenham had succeeded in getting away with over a quarter of a million pounds worth of unset diamonds But, although he had caught the robber, he had failed to recover the proceeds of the robbery. What had happened to these Wenham had steadfastly refused to disclose. He remained obstinate throughout his trial, and continued to remain obstinate after he had been sentenced and transferred to Dartmoor, although Mr.

Budd had had more interviews with him on the subject than he cared to remember.

Now, with the man lying seriously ill in the prison infirmary, he was on his way to try once more, with no very great hopes that he would be successful.

'That feller's a long time, isn't he?' he remarked, breaking a period of silence.

'P'raps he's lost himself and can't find his way back to the car,' suggested Leek.

'Perhaps he's gone up in a balloon!' snarled Mr. Budd. 'Couldn't 'ave lost himself, the lights 'ud guide 'im.'

He listened, but no sound reached his ears. The same fog-deadened silence surrounded them on all sides. The stout man leaned forward with difficulty and, wiping the moisture off the glass of the window with his hand, peered out. But he could see nothing. The swirling mist was impenetrable and seemed, if anything, to have grown denser.

'It looks to me as if we're here for the night,' he remarked, sinking back into his corner, 'so we'd better make the best of it.'

Sergeant Leek's face lengthened. So far as he could see there was no 'best' to be made. He was cold and hungry. The prospect of spending the long night huddled up in the car was not alluring. The mist might clear, but there seemed very little hope of that — before morning, at any rate.

The sergeant was still commiserating with himself over the harshness of life when he heard a sound, a faint, muffled cry, that came from somewhere out in the void of fog-filled darkness.

Mr. Budd heard it, too, and opening his eyes sat up.

'What was that?' he muttered.

'It sounded like a cry,' said Leek, who was mentally incapable of saying anything but the obvious.

'I didn't think it was a prima-donna practising top notes!' grunted the stout man. 'I wonder if Spencer's hurt himself.'

His hand was on the handle of the door and he had partly opened it when another sound reached him. From out of the fog came faint, stumbling footsteps. They were barely audible at first, but grew louder as they came nearer. A figure, swaying and unsteady, staggered out of the curtain of fog into the light of the headlamps. It stumbled forward, almost fell, recovered itself, and then collapsed across the long radiator.

'Spencer!' grunted Mr. Budd, who had caught a glimpse of the man's agonised face.

With an agility that was remarkable for a man of his size he was out of the car and round to the side of the sprawling figure of the police driver before Leek had sufficiently recovered from his surprise to move.

Spencer had fallen limply across the bonnet, and when Mr. Budd bent over him his clawing fingers were clutching spasmodically at the varnished paintwork.

'What's the matter?' asked the stout Superintendent, attempting to raise the man.

He mumbled something, shivered, and his working fingers ceased to move.

'What's happened? Is he ill?' asked Leek anxiously as he came to the side of his superior.

'He's dead!' answered Mr. Budd soberly, and looked at his hands in the light of the car's lamps.

They were covered in blood!

2

The house on the moor

Sergeant Leek's breath left his lips in a shocked gasp and his eyes opened very wide.

'Where — where did that come from?' he stammered feebly.

Mr. Budd, still looking at his stained hands, replied without turning his head.

'From Spencer,' he said, 'when I tried to lift him.'

'But — but — ' Leek's voice, a little shaky, stopped as Mr. Budd straightened up suddenly.

'Help me shift him on to the grass,' said the stout man, and between them they lifted the still form of the police driver and laid him gently by the side of the car. 'Feel in his pockets and see if you can find the torch,' ordered Mr. Budd, wiping his hands on his handkerchief.

The sergeant obeyed and produced it.

Pressing the button he focused the dead man in a circle of light. Thrusting the handkerchief back in his pocket Mr. Budd dropped on to one knee.

'That's where the blood came from.' he said, and pointed to a narrow slit on the left side of the coat. 'He's been stabbed!'

'Stabbed?' The word whistled through Leek's clenched teeth. 'But — it's impossible!'

'Nothin's impossible that happens,' grunted Mr. Budd, and began to unbutton the dead man's coat and waistcoat.

They were soaked with blood, and when he pulled aside the shirt and laid bare the chest they saw the wound from which it had come.

'Stabbed!' repeated the stout Superintendent, and his big face was set sternly.

Leek, amazed, incredulous, a little fearful, stared uneasily into the mist.

'Who — who could have stabbed him?' he muttered in a low voice.

Mr. Budd shook his head, slowly.

'I dunno,' he replied. 'Somebody did — somebody out there in the fog.'

The sergeant gave a little shiver. There was something particularly unpleasant in the thought that somewhere, concealed by that dense white vapour, was a killer

'What had we better do?' he asked.

The stout Superintendent rose to his feet and took the torch from his hand.

'You stay here,' he said. 'I'm goin' to see if I can find anythin'.'

Leek choked down the protest that rose to his lips. The prospect of being left alone with a dead man, with the murderer lurking close at hand, did not appeal to him at all. He thought it wiser, however, to say nothing, and watched the stout figure of his superior melt into the mist.

Mr. Budd, the light of the torch directed on the ground at his feet, advanced slowly in the direction from which he had heard the cry that had been the herald of the tragedy. Visibility was appalling. Three yards in front of him he could see nothing and his progress was slow in consequence.

Suddenly and unexpectedly there loomed up before him a wall. He stopped and turned his light on it. It was a brick wall, obviously old. It rose out of the ground and was lost in the foggy darkness. Standing on tiptoe he reached up and felt about for the top but he couldn't find it. The wall, therefore, must be fairly high.

The fact that there was a wall suggested the nearby presence of a house and after a pause the stout Superintendent set off to explore.

That vague mumble which had come from Spencer's lips just before he died had been unintelligible except for two words, which Mr. Budd had caught distinctly. 'The black — ' something or other.

What had the dying man been trying to say? Had he striven with his last breath to supply a clue to his murderer? Mr. Budd was puzzled.

The black — what? What had come out of the fog and stricken him down? And for what reason had he been killed?

The fat detective tried to find some satisfactory theory as he followed the course of the wall, but he was unsuccessful. He could think of nothing to suggest a reason for Spencer's death or explain those last words: the black — what?

The wall stopped abruptly, ending in a brick pillar on which swung a gate. The gate had once been white but was now of a nondescript hue from long exposure to the weather. It was half open, and beyond was the gravelled mouth of a drive.

Mr. Budd ran his light along the top bar of the gate and came upon a name in faded black letters. Moor Lodge. So the suggestion offered by the wall was right. Somewhere beyond the fog-swathed drive was a house

Mr. Budd pursed his lips. Was the place occupied or empty? If it was occupied it seemed scarcely likely that its inhabitants could have had anything to do with the killing of an inoffensive police officer. And yet they may have heard something . . .

The big man came to a decision. Turning his light on the path he began to make his way up the drive.

Twice he came to an unexpected bend and stumbling over a grass edging found himself in the midst of a thick, clammy shrubbery. The same uncanny stillness surrounded him here as it had done on the open moor. There was no sound at all except the faint crunching of his own footsteps on the wet gravel. The fog seemed to act as a muffler, deadening the sense of hearing as well as blotting out sight.

The approach to the house seemed endless, and it argued that the place to which it gave admittance must be fairly large. And presently he came upon it, the first warning that he was near being provided by a dim glimmer of light that filtered through the mist. It marked the location of a porch.

The ray from his torch showed him a shallow flight of stone steps, worn and lichen-stained. He mounted them to a recessed front door, found the wrought-iron knocker, and knocked. There was no reply. But for the dim light that glowed behind the stained glass panels of the door the house might have been empty.

Mr. Budd frowned, allowed a short interval to elapse, and then repeated his summons, this time louder and more peremptory.

'They're bound to hear that,' he

thought, stepping back and gently stroking the lowest of his many chins But it produced no more effect than his previous knocking.

Mr. Budd grunted. It was barely eight o'clock. They couldn't have gone to bed. Perhaps they were all at dinner somewhere in the back of the house But even then surely a servant would be on duty. Perhaps there was a bell . . .

He had put out his torch after safely negotiating the steps and his thumb was on the button, preparatory to switching it on again to look for a possible bell-push, when, with surprising suddenness the door was jerked open.

'Put up your hands!' snapped a voice, and Mr. Budd found himself staring into the muzzle of an automatic gripped in the hand of a youthful looking man in plus fours who stood on the threshold.

3

The inhabitants of the house

'Put that thing away,' said the stout Superintendent sternly. 'I'm a police officer, and if you start foolin' round you'll get into trouble.'

Across the face of the man in the doorway flickered an expression of surprise, but he made no attempt to lower the weapon he held.

'A police officer, are you?' he said. 'Then what are you doing here on a night like this?'

'I'm investigating a serious crime,' said Mr. Budd in his best official manner. 'Put that gun away!'

The young man — the Superintendent judged him to be somewhere in the early thirties — still hesitated.

'How am I to know you're a police officer?' he asked suspiciously.

Mr. Budd sighed wearily, plunged his

hand into his breast pocket, took out a wallet and produced his warrant card.

'That ought to satisfy you, if you can read!' he grunted.

The other frowned, peered at the card, and lowered the threatening pistol.

'Sorry,' he said briefly. 'But I wasn't taking any risks.'

The stout Superintendent sniffed.

'Do you usually greet visitors with a gun?' he asked.

The man in plus fours smiled and shook his head.

'No,' he answered. 'But somebody tried to break in here earlier tonight and I thought when you knocked — well, I thought it might be a gag.'

Mr. Budd's eyes narrowed.

'Somebody tried to break in, did they?' he asked, slowly. 'When was this?'

'About half an hour ago,' was the reply.

'H'm!' said the stout man. His lids drooped over his eyes until they were almost completely closed. He was not easily surprised, but his reception and the explanation for it had certainly supplied him with something to think about. 'Did you see anything of this person who tried to break in?' he murmured.

'My wife did,' answered the other, and then curiously: 'It wasn't that which brought you here?'

'No, sir,' Mr. Budd shook his head. 'Murder brought me here!'

'Murder!' gasped the questioner. 'Was that the serious crime you mentioned?'

'It was,' said the Superintendent. 'If you can tell me anythin' more serious I'll be glad to hear it.'

'Good Lord!' exclaimed the young man. 'Where did this happen? Who was killed?'

Mr. Budd told him, and he listened, his face anxious and concerned.

'Dreadful!' he breathed. 'D'you think this fellow who tried to get into the house can have done it?'

'I don't think nothin'!' said the Superintendent. 'I'd like to have a word with your wife though, sir.'

'Is that necessary?' asked the other, and then, before Mr. Budd could reply: 'Yes, of course, I suppose it is. You'd better come in.'

He stood aside as the big man ponderously crossed the threshold.

'If you'll wait here for a moment,' he went on, 'I'll just have a word with my wife and tell her why you're here.'

He closed the door, crossed the hall, and entered a room on the left. Mr. Budd heard the faint murmur of voices and while he was waiting took stock of his surroundings.

The hall was large and almost square. Facing the front door was a big staircase that led upwards into deep shadow. The furniture was old and, he noted with surprise, indescribably dusty. The oak parquet of the floor had seen neither a broom nor polish for many a day. He was puzzling over the reason for this when the man in plus fours came back and enlightened him.

'I've told my wife,' he said, 'and she's naturally a little nervous. I'm afraid you'll have to forgive the state of the house. We only arrived here this morning from abroad.'

'Oh, I see,' murmured Mr. Budd. 'Can I have your name, sir, please?'

'Garland. James Garland,' said the young man pleasantly. 'Come this way, Superintendent, and I hope you won't alarm my wife more than is necessary. She has already had one shock which has rather upset her.'

He led the way across to the room that he had entered before and opened the door, motioning Mr. Budd to precede him. The room was large and furnished in the same old-fashioned style as the hall. Here, too, the dust was thick, and there were signs of neglect. A small fire burned in the rusty grate and in front of this was seated a pretty, fair-haired girl.

'This is Superintendent Budd, of Scotland Yard, dear,' said Garland. 'My wife, Superintendent. She'll tell you anything she can.'

The girl smiled nervously. She was frightened and uneasy, and her small hands played restlessly with a handkerchief in her lap.

'What is it you want to know?' she asked in a low voice, and from the faint accent Mr. Budd concluded that she was an American.

'I'm interested in this attempt to break in, Mrs. Garland,' he said. 'I understand you saw the man.'

She nodded and shivered.

'Yes, I saw him,' she answered. 'He was at the kitchen window.'

'What was he like? Can you give me a description of him?' said the big man, but she shook her head.

'No, I only saw him for a minute,' she replied.

'I'd gone into the kitchen to cook a meal. The light wasn't on, and as I pressed the switch I heard a sound at the window. The curtains weren't drawn and I saw something outside. It looked like a man with something over his face. I was scared and I flew back here and told my husband. He went out at once to see if he could see anything, but there was nothing.'

'Then when you knocked,' put in Garland, 'I thought that having failed to get in one way he was trying another.'

'Burglars don't usually knock at doors,' murmured Mr. Budd thoughtfully. 'Neither do they usually choose such an early

129

hour to begin operations. You only came here this morning, you say?'

Garland nodded.

'Yes,' he answered. 'And we haven't got any servants or anything yet. It was because of this that my wife was so frightened. We were quite alone in the house and it's a big place and rather isolated.'

'You see,' explained Mrs. Garland, 'we only arrived from New York yesterday.'

Mr. Budd raised his eyebrows.

'Only yesterday,' he murmured. 'You must have moved pretty quickly to get this house in the time.'

Garland smiled faintly.

'The house is mine,' he answered. 'You see I was born here. But when my people died, about ten years ago, I shut it up and went to America.'

'H'm!' The stout Superintendent scratched his chin. 'And you didn't come back till yesterday. I should have thought it 'ud have been better to stop the night in an hotel till the place was properly prepared for you.'

'We expected the servants would be

here,' said the girl. 'Jim cabled to an agency to engage them before we left New York. I wish we hadn't come here now.'

The big man was thoughtful. Who was this mysterious individual who had tried to break in? Not an ordinary burglar, evidently. His methods were not in accordance with those generally adopted by members of his fraternity. Some tramp perhaps who thought the house was empty and was looking for somewhere to shelter from the fog. And yet a tramp wouldn't have gone to the length of murder. It was a queer business. There must be some connection between the man Mrs. Garland had seen and the death of Spencer. It was unlikely that the attempt to break into Moor Lodge and the murder were unrelated. That kind of coincidence didn't happen.

'Have you any idea,' he said, breaking the silence, 'why this man should have wanted to get into the house?'

Garland shook his head.

'Not the faintest,' he answered. 'There's nothing of any great value here, as you can see for yourself.'

'And the house has been empty ever since you went to America ten years ago?' said Mr. Budd.

'No,' corrected Garland. 'It was let furnished six years ago to a man called Kingsley. He died here.'

'Oh, he died here,' said the Superintendent. 'When was this?'

'About three years ago,' answered Garland.

'You saw nothing when you went out, after Mrs. Garland's fright?' inquired Mr. Budd.

'No,' said Garland. 'I saw nothing. It wouldn't have been easy to see much in this fog.'

'No, I suppose not,' agreed the big man.

'I made a circuit of the house,' went on the other, 'and came in.'

'And you heard nothing?' said Mr. Budd. 'After you got in.'

'Nothing at all!' declared Garland.

'And that's all you can tell me?' His tone was disappointed. 'Well, I think I'll be getting back to my sergeant and the car. He'll be wondering what's happened to me.'

'What are you going to do?' asked the girl nervously.

'I can't do any more tonight, ma'am,' said Mr. Budd. 'There's no sign of the fog liftin', and until it does we can't move.'

'You'd better take pot-luck with us,' suggested Garland. 'It's not very cheerful here, but at least there's something to eat. It's better than spending the night out in the fog.'

'Thank you very much, sir,' said Mr. Budd. 'I'll be glad to accept your offer. I'll just go and notify my sergeant and come back.'

He bowed to the girl and Garland followed him into the hall.

'There's a garage at the back of the house,' he whispered. 'I didn't want to mention it before my wife but perhaps you'd — you'd care to bring that poor fellow — ' He left the sentence, unfinished, but Mr. Budd gathered what he meant and nodded.

'I was goin' to suggest somethin' like that,' he said, and went out into the fog.

His thoughts as he made his way slowly down the twisting drive by the light of his torch were confused. What had happened in the vicinity of that lonely house during the last hour? Who was the man whom the girl had seen outside the kitchen window, and what had been the meaning of Spencer's last words? What had the man meant by 'the black'?

'Peculiar and interestin',' murmured the stout detective as he reached the gate. 'Queer, too! People don't commit murder except for a very good reason. And why anyone should have wanted to kill poor Spencer I'm hanged if I know!'

He came out of the drive and paused. The crime must have been committed somewhere quite close to where he was standing. Spencer, groping around in the fog had come upon someone and been killed because — because what? Had he heard or seen something that rendered his death necessary for someone's safety? And what had he seen which had put into his mind those two words mumbled almost inaudibly before he died — 'the black'.

Mr. Budd sighed and continued wearily towards the spot where he had left Leek and the stationary car. But a second shock awaited him, for he could find no sign of it. No faint ray from the headlights penetrated the misty darkness.

He thought he might have misjudged his directions and called, but there was no answer.

For twenty minutes he searched about. Presently he found a bloodstain on the rough ground; a bloodstain that he concluded marked the place where he and Leek had laid the body of Spencer. But the body was no longer there, neither was the car, neither was Leek. They had all three disappeared as completely as though a giant hand had come out of the foggy night and snatched them from the face of the earth.

4

A very queer business

Mr. Budd stood, surrounded by the damp, clammy wreathes of swirling fog, and stared at the place where he had left Leek with the car and the dead man such a short time ago. What could have happened to them? The lean sergeant could not drive, and even if he had been able to would never have attempted to move the car on such a night. There was no reason why he should and every reason why he should not.

The stout Superintendent fondled his triple chin and frowned. He was perplexed and uneasy. What had occurred at this desolate spot while he had been interviewing the people at Moor Lodge?

He stooped with difficulty and, in the light of the torch, made a careful examination of the ground in the hope that he would find something to explain this extraordinary disappearance. The smear of blood on the coarse grass was plainly visible, testifying that he had made no mistake in the place. And if further evidence was needed a short distance away he could distinctly see the impressions made by the tyres of the standing car. There was a confused jumble of footprints, but no signs of a struggle. If Leek, waiting there alone for his return, had been attacked he had been taken by surprise.

It was pretty obvious that the car had been driven off, and he attempted to follow the tracks, but, beyond the grass edging, the road was hard and further traces became invisible.

A little breathless from his exertions, he straightened up. There could be little doubt that someone had attacked Leek and after rendering him unconscious, or worse, driven away with him and the dead man. But why? Was there a lunatic at large, a homicidal maniac who had escaped under cover of the fog from some nearby asylum or nursing home? It seemed impossible to account for the recent happenings in any other way. Surely no sane person would have committed murder for no apparent reason?

It was an unpleasant thought that perhaps somewhere lurking behind that screen of vapour was a crazy man with a lust for killing. Mr. Budd, and not for the first time in his career, wished that police regulations made it customary for a detective to carry a pistol, but police regulations frowned on such a practice. Only on very rare occasions was such a thing permitted, and then only after a great deal of red tape. The hard butt of an automatic would, he thought, have been very comforting just then.

He thrust his hand into the breast of his overcoat, found the top pocket of his waistcoat, and withdrew one of his long, black cigars. With the end between his teeth he searched for and found his match-box, struck a match, and when the cigar was alight drew in the smoke gratefully. He felt he needed a solace.

There was nothing for it but to go back to the house. He could do no good where he was. To attempt any further search was simply a waste of time. He began to move heavily towards the gate, hoping that his sense of direction would not lead him astray.

The silence was oppressive, and he found himself wondering how long the fog would last. Sometimes these dense mists obscured the moors for several days. He hoped this was not one of the times. The blanketing whiteness was getting on his nerves.

He found the gate after some little difficulty. Although he had been under the impression he was making a straight line for it he discovered in reality that he had deviated by nearly fifty yards.

For the second time that night he started up the drive. He had rounded the first bend when he heard a sound that brought him to a stop. It was the faint rustling of leaves, and it came from the shrubbery on his left.

Switching out his torch he stood motionless, listening. Again the faint noise reached his ears. Was it caused by someone concealed among the bushes or just the passing of an animal? He waited for several seconds. The sound was not repeated, and once more putting on his light he moved forward.

When he reached the porch he saw to his surprise that the front door stood open. Probably Garland had come out to see if there were any signs of his return. He mounted the steps laboriously and stood within the open doorway for a moment before advancing further into the hall. No one came out to greet him, and believing that possibly they had not heard his approach he went over to the door of the room to which Garland had taken him before and knocked softly. Receiving no reply he twisted the handle and looked in. The fire was still burning in the rusty grate but the room was empty. Possibly they were getting a meal in some other part of the house.

He retreated to the hall again and called.

'Mr. Garland!' His voice echoed, but nobody answered.

The big man was not of a nervous disposition, but as he stood in the square hall and waited for a reply to his hail he felt a nasty creepy sensation in the region of his spine.

'Mr. Garland!' He called again louder, but it had no more effect than before.

Mr. Budd's lips compressed and his heavy jowls tautened. Where were the two people whom he had left in the house a little while ago?

He went over to the staircase and looked up into the gloom. It was impossible they could not have heard him. He called a third time, with the same negative result.

'This is gettin' monotonous,' he muttered. 'First Leek disappears, now these people seem to have done the same.'

A thought struck him. He remembered the open door. Could they, for some reason or other, have gone out? Perhaps they had heard some sound although it seemed unlikely that the girl would have gone too. Still, it was a possibility.

He went to the top of the steps and peered out into the darkness, listening intently, but no sound greeted his straining ears. Descending the shallow steps he called Garland's name again, but his voice was thrown back to him from the fog and nobody answered.

He re-entered the house and shut the door deliberately. Something very queer was happening that night. Something, that for the first time in his life, made the stout Superintendent feel scared.

He shook off that momentary qualm of fear and with his cigar gripped tightly between his teeth began a search of the house. He started with the room in which the fire burned, and here he made a discovery. One of the worn and faded rugs had been kicked aside and when he straightened it he discovered on the dusty floor a red smear. It was blood, and when he gingerly applied his fingertips he found it was still wet.

His face was grave as he stared at the ominous stain. What had taken place in this room while he had gone in search of Leek? Whose blood had left that sinister smear on the dusty boards?

He continued an examination of the room without finding anything else of importance and turned his attention to the rest of the house. It took an effort of will to leave the lighted room after what he had found. There was no knowing what might lie concealed in the shadowy ramifications of Moor Lodge. He explored the whole of the ground floor. Apart from the big kitchen and the scullery there were three other rooms, excluding the one in which he had found the bloodstain. On the table in the kitchen he saw some packages of food and a loaf of bread. A fire burned in the big range and the kettle was singing on the top. The other rooms were dark and tenantless, the furniture still swathed in dustsheets.

He came to the foot of the staircase and looked up into the uninviting shadows that concealed the landing, hesitating for a second before he resolutely began to climb.

The carpetless stairs creaked under his weight and once, as he neared the top, he thought he heard a movement above, but when he paused to listen only silence reached him. The stairs emerged on to a square landing, almost equal in size to the hall.

Standing in the centre of this he sent the light of his torch flashing round. Like the rest of the house this upper part was dusty and neglected. He saw several closed doors and going to the first one opened it and peeped into the room beyond. It was a large bedroom. An old-fashioned four-poster bed occupied the centre of one wall and there were various other articles of furniture.

The stout man assured himself that there was no one there and went to the next door.

From room to room he went until he had exhausted the whole of that floor, and then moved up the staircase to the next, but he found no one. The house, except for himself, was empty. Garland and his wife had, like Leek and the body of Spencer, vanished into the unknown.

5

The figure in black

It was uncanny and not a little alarming. Mr. Budd was phlegmatic and not in the least given to neurotic imaginings, but there was something intensely eerie in the thought that he was entirely alone in that house in the vicinity of which, such a short time before, a man had come violently by his death. Not only alone but completely cut off, owing to the fog, from communication with the outside world, for there was no telephone. It was one of the first things he had looked for, and although he would have been surprised if there had been one, its absence provided the final touch to this feeling of complete isolation.

He went into the only habitable room and stirred the dying fire to a blaze. There was some coal in a box at the side of the fender and he threw several lumps on, concluding he might as well be warm if nothing else.

Twisting a chair round so that it was in such a position that he could see both the window and the door he sat down heavily to think out the inexplicable situation in which he found himself.

Something very strange had taken place in that house and its immediate neighbourhood. Where was Leek and the dead man? What had happened to Garland and the girl? Why, during the short time he had been absent, had they been spirited away?

His eyes sought the blood smear on the floor. From that it looked as though there had been violence. He remembered Garland's revolver. The man had evidently had no opportunity to use it. Even the fog could scarcely have deadened the sound of a shot. If the weapon had been fired he would have heard the report while he was searching for Leek and the car. The Garlands must therefore have been taken by surprise, as, from the evidence of the ground, the sergeant had been. It seemed that there must be more than one person in this business. But what was the business?

He flung away the stub of his cigar, took out another, and lighted it, flicking the used match into the fireplace. Once more his thoughts returned to Spencer's last words: 'the black — '

The man had seen something, either before or at the moment the knife had entered his breast, to put those words into his mind. What?

He jerked up, suddenly alert, listening, his eyes turned towards the mist obscured window. Had it been his imagination or was the sound that had reached him a stealthy footstep?

It came again, the soft pad of feet, but this time from outside the door. He turned swiftly and could have sworn that the handle moved.

The short hairs on his thick neck rose, but he mastered that momentary panic, crossed swiftly to the door and jerked it open. The hall was empty.

'Beginnin' to get nervy in me old age,' he muttered.

Closing the door he came back to his

chair to resume his interrupted thoughts. But he had barely reseated himself when he heard a fresh sound. This time distinct, unmistakable, the sound of someone walking across the floor of the room above.

He went quickly to the door, opened it noiselessly, and tiptoeing across the hall listened at the foot of the staircase.

Silence!

As quietly as he could he mounted to the first landing. The door of the room above the one in which he had been seated was open. When he had made his search he distinctly remembered having closed it.

'Who's there?' he called sharply, but nobody answered.

He took out his torch, pressed the button, and sent a ray of light sweeping into the darkened room. It picked out the various items of furniture but nothing else.

Overcoming a sudden dread he entered boldly and made a closer inspection. The room was empty!

There were little beads of perspiration

standing out on his big face as he came out and closed the door behind him. Drawing out his handkerchief he mopped them away. Somebody had been in that room. There was somebody besides himself in that apparently deserted house. Doors did not open of their own accord and footsteps were only made by human feet.

He forced himself to look into the other rooms, but there was nobody hiding there. They were as empty as when he had searched them before.

'This is gettin' me down,' he muttered. 'What is at the bottom of this Maskelyne and Devant stuff?'

He walked to the head of the staircase with the intention of descending once more to the hall and nearly cried out as something brushed passed his arm and struck the stair below him with a thud.

Stooping he plucked the quivering thing from where it had stuck in the woodwork. It was a long, thin knife and the blade was dark with blood.

Someone had sent it hurtling down from the floor above!

Mr. Budd switched out his torch and pressing himself against the wall listened in the hope of hearing some sound of his concealed enemy. But he heard nothing. After the thud made by the knife striking, the stillness was undisturbed.

The position was, to say the least of it, uncomfortable. Somewhere in the darkness of the upper landing lurked an unknown person whose reactions to Mr. Budd were not favourable. An inch or so's difference in the direction of the knife and it would not have stuck harmlessly in the stair.

The big man decided that in the circumstances discretion was undoubtedly the better part of valour. He had, it was true, accidentally been supplied with a weapon, but it was useless, except at close quarters, and he had no means of knowing what other armaments the unknown possessed. Garland had owned a revolver. It was unlikely that it had been left in his keeping. It would be merely foolhardy, therefore, to attempt an investigation into the shadowy realms of the floor above. He would only be offering himself as a target.

He began to edge his way softly down the stairs, moving cautiously with his back against the wall and trying to avoid making the treads creak. It was slow progress, but he reached the hall at last and expelled his pent-up breath in relief. That moment on the top of the staircase had tried his nerves to the utmost.

Crossing quickly to the lighted room with the fire he entered it, this time leaving the door open so that he could see the wide expanse of the hall. Anyone approaching the room would have to cross that brightly lit area, and it would be impossible to take him by surprise.

Standing in front of the fireplace with his back to the fire he inspected the knife that had dropped so perilously close. There was little doubt that it was the weapon that had killed Spencer. The smeared stains on the sharp blade were still tacky. Mr. Budd smiled a trifle grimly and altogether mirthlessly. His discovery meant that the killer was in the house, and his anxiety concerning the whereabouts of Garland and his wife increased. So, incidentally, did his concern for his own safety. The mysterious person or persons who were concentrating their energies on the old house that night had the place to themselves except for him, and that he was a stumbling block to their plans, whatever they might be, was proved by the episode of the knife.

He tried to imagine what lay behind this business, but his imagination failed to supply him with a reasonable explanation.

Mechanically his fingers searched in his waistcoat pocket for another of his inevitable cigars, but he had smoked the last.

A creak reached his ears and he stiffened. The creak had come from the direction of the staircase. Somebody was descending!

He watched the lighted hall expectantly. Again he heard the sound, and then, the light beyond the door went out.

Mr. Budd drew in his breath sharply and his fingers closed more tightly round the hilt of the knife he still held. Somewhere in the now dark hall somebody was moving stealthily. With narrowed eyes he stared at the patch of blackness that marked the oblong of the open door, but he saw nothing.

A minute passed in dead silence, and then, out of the darkness came a hand.

The stout Superintendent felt a sudden chill. The hand crept round the jamb of the door and began to grope for the light switch. He could see nothing of the person to whom the hand belonged, except part of a black-clad arm.

The sliding fingers had almost reached the switch when he acted. It was a good distance from the fireplace to the door but he covered it in two bounds and gripped the wrist of the unknown owner of that searching hand.

There was a muttered exclamation. For an instant, in the light that streamed through the doorway, he caught a glimpse of a black shape; black from head to foot, with no break in the sombre hue to mark the face. And then before he could tear the fingers away they had pressed the switch. The light behind him went out and he found himself struggling desperately with his unknown assailant in the red glow from the fire.

6

The knocking

The man was strong and as difficult to hold as an eel. A foot twined round the back of one of Mr. Budd's ankles and a quick jerk sent him crashing backwards to the floor. The elbow of his right arm came in violent contact with the bare boards and the knife that he held flew from his numbed grasp.

The figure in black flung himself upon him. He felt hands at his throat. He caught a momentary vision of glaring eyes and yellow-white teeth in a mask of black, and in spite of the strangling grasp on his throat Spencer's last words flashed to his mind: 'the black', and he knew now what the man had been trying to say.

He tried to tear the choking grip from his throat as he felt his senses reeling, but the strength of the man above him was colossal. The red glow of the fire merged into a reddish mist flecked with brighter flashes, and then as he realized he must breathe or die there came a loud peremptory knocking.

The stranglehold relaxed. Mr. Budd drew a gasping lungful of air and wrenched the murderer's hands from his throat. The knocking came again. Somebody was at the front door seeking admittance.

The black man, alarmed, sprang to his feet and disappeared into the darkness of the hall. Mr. Budd, breathing stertorously and tenderly caressing his fat neck, scrambled ponderously up. Stooping, he retrieved the knife and turning to the switch pressed it down, experiencing a feeling of relief as the light came on. There was something comforting in light.

He was shaken and a little dizzy, but determined to find out who had knocked. Still retaining the knife he pulled out his torch and sent a ray of light to illumine the hall, and when, by its aid, he had assured himself that his recent assailant was nowhere in the immediate vicinity, sidled cautiously towards the front door.

He dared not turn his back on the shadowy hall in case his unknown adversary should renew his attack.

There was another assault on the knocker as he reached the door, and pulling back the catch he jerked it open, flashing his light on to the person who stood in the porch. It was Leek!

'Excuse me — ' began the sergeant, blinking in the sudden glare, and Mr. Budd, for once in his life, was heartily glad to hear that melancholy voice.

'Come in,' he said, before Leek could complete his polite inquiry, 'and look sharp. There's sudden death lurking about this house!'

The sergeant gaped stupidly.

'Oh, it's you!' he exclaimed in surprise. 'What are you doin' here?'

'Playin' hide-and-seek!' snapped Mr. Budd. 'Come inside.'

Leek obeyed, and the big man slammed the door.

'There's a switch somewhere over by the foot of the stairs that works this light,' he went on, directing the torch towards the spot he mentioned. 'Go and see if you can find it and put it on.'

'What — ' Leek started a plaintive question, but Mr. Budd interrupted him.

'Don't start arguin'!' he snarled, and his subordinate resignedly went to do his bidding.

He found the switch and the hall light came on. It revealed Mr. Budd's dishevelled appearance, and Leek stared in wonder.

'What's been 'appenin'?' he demanded. 'You look a bit queer.'

'You wouldn't look so good if you'd been nearly strangled,' growled his superior. 'Or maybe in your case it 'ud be an improvement!'

'Nearly strangled?' echoed the sergeant, his lean face incredulous. 'Who did that?'

'I dunno!' The stout man glared at the shadowy staircase. 'Some feller who's playin' funny tricks here — and not so funny, either. If I get my hands on the — '

He stopped abruptly and led the way into the room in which his recent struggle with the unknown had taken place.

'Now,' he continued, as the shivering Leek warmed his hands gratefully at the fire, 'where have you been?'

'Walkin' round in circles,' answered the sergeant miserably.

Mr. Budd grunted.

'What happened to the car and Spencer's body?' he asked. 'What d'you mean by 'walkin' round in circles', when I left you to look after him?'

'Well, it was like this,' explained the sergeant, in an injured voice. 'After you'd gone I sat down on the runnin' board of the car waitin' for you to come back. I didn't think you was goin' to be long. After a bit I heard somebody callin' in the fog, and thinkin' it was you and maybe you'd found somethin' I went towards the sound of the voice. I couldn't find no one and I called. Somebody answered me from further away, in a different direction. I must have gone further than I thought, for presently I 'eard the sound of the car startin'. I couldn't see nothin' for the fog, and then the noise of the engine stopped and I 'ad nothin' to guide me. What with the darkness and the fog I didn't know where I was.'

'Didn't you hear me call?' demanded

Mr. Budd. 'When I came back and found you and the car and Spencer gone I shouted.'

'I didn't hear nothin',' replied Leek. 'I must 'ave been out of earshot by then. I believe I walked miles out there in the mist before I stumbled by accident on the gate of this house. I thought maybe the people livin' 'ere 'ud be able to tell me where I was, so I came and knocked. I never expected to find you 'ere, though.' He looked round at the dusty room, his face puzzled. 'What 'as been 'appenin'?' he asked. 'Who lives 'ere?'

'Nobody, apparently,' answered Mr. Budd, and told him what had occurred.

Leek scratched his long chin.

'Funny business, ain't it?' he muttered. 'Who's this black feller and what did he want to kill Spencer for?'

'How should I know,' replied the stout Superintendent irritably. 'I dunno anythin' about it. I only know those two people have disappeared and that there's somebody loose about this house who's not particular about a murder or two.'

Leek looked uneasily towards the door.

'You mean this feller's still on the premises?' he asked.

'Of course he's on the premises,' said Mr. Budd. 'Your knockin' scared him for the moment and he's gone back to his lair upstairs. The only electric bulbs in this house are in the hall and in here, and as long as he keeps above he's safe enough.'

'I wonder what the idea is?' muttered the sergeant.

'The idea,' said Mr. Budd, 'is that for some reason or other this feller wants the house to himself, but why, I don't know.'

He stooped laboriously to straighten the rug, which the struggle with the unknown had rumpled. As he did so he caught sight of an oblong slip of paper which had not been there before. Picking it up he looked at it, read with a puzzled frown the three words scrawled in pencil across it, and handed it to Leek.

'What d'you make of that?' he asked.

The lugubrious sergeant took it.

'"The Black Widow",' he read aloud. 'Queer, what does it mean?'

'I was askin' you that,' said Mr. Budd. 'Must have slipped out of that feller's pocket when he was massaging my throat.'

'P'raps it's the name of a pub,' suggested Leek.

'P'raps it's me grandmother's maiden aunt!' snarled Mr. Budd. 'Why should the man carry the name of a pub about with him?'

'Why shouldn't he?' argued the sergeant. 'Maybe he's got an appointment to meet somebody there.'

Mr. Budd made no reply. He was thinking. In spite of his scoffing rejection of Leek's idea there might be something in it, although at the back of his mind the words on the paper seemed more likely to connect in some vague way with the black face he had glimpsed in the firelight. Something he had meant to put into practice before occurred to him and he turned to Leek.

'Never mind worrying about that now,' he said. 'Garland mentioned there was a garage at the side of the house, and I want to have a look at it. I haven't had an opportunity before, but now you're here I can. So far as I can see that's the only place these people can have been taken to.'

Leek looked dubious.

'You're not going to leave me here alone, are you?' he said in alarm.

'Why not?' demanded Mr. Budd.

'Well,' said the sergeant, 'suppose this feller starts any funny business.'

'You can laugh!' said the Superintendent calmly. 'I had to stay here alone, and I don't see any reason why you shouldn't.'

'You'd better let me come with you,' said Leek. 'I don't see any sense in stopping here.'

Mr. Budd had opened his mouth to deliver a scathing reply when, without warning, the light flickered and went out.

'Who did that?' gasped Leek, in the semi-darkness.

Mr. Budd saw that the hall light had also gone out and guessed what had happened.

'That feller's either found the main switch or pulled a fuse,' he muttered. 'Look out for squalls. I think the next few minutes are goin' to be excitin'.'

7

The attack

With nerves and muscles braced the stout Superintendent waited for the next move on the part of the unknown occupant of Moor Lodge, and it was a long time coming. After that sudden descent of darkness nothing happened.

The silence was unbroken, except for the irregular breathing of Leek near him. Dimly, in the faint red glow of the fire, he could make out the lean figure of the sergeant, tense and expectant, his face turned towards the black gulf that marked the hall.

Quietly Mr. Budd reached towards the mantelpiece where he had laid the knife and slid his thick fingers round the hilt. It was the only weapon between them, and might prove useful.

A minute dragged slowly by — one of the longest minutes the big man had ever experienced — and still the mysterious unknown gave no sign of his existence.

Mr. Budd fingered the torch in his pocket suppressing by an effort a strong desire to send a ray of light through the blackness beyond the door that welled up within him. The urge to find out what that blackness concealed was almost overpowering.

The attack, when at last it came, was sudden and from a totally unexpected quarter.

With a scraping screech the window went up behind them, and as they both swung round they caught sight of a dim figure framed in the opening.

'Stick 'em up!' rasped a husky voice. 'Go on, look slippy unless you want a dose of lead in you!'

The stout man saw the menacing muzzle of a pistol held in the gloved hand and decided that argument was futile. Slowly he raised his fat arms, and Leek, his mouth still open from his astonishment, followed suit.

'That's better!' growled the man at the window approvingly. 'Now drop that knife! Quick!'

Mr. Budd opened his fingers and the released weapon fell with a clatter to the floor.

'Who are you?' he demanded calmly.

'Never mind who I am!' snapped the newcomer. 'You keep still and do as you're told, otherwise it 'ull be the worse for you! Are you there, Harry?'

'Yes,' grunted a second voice, and out of the corner of his eye Mr. Budd saw another man shuffle into the room.

'Come and take this,' said the one at the window and keep 'em covered while I climb in.'

The man he had addressed as Harry crossed quickly towards him, carefully keeping out of the line of fire, and took the pistol from his hand. The exchange was made so rapidly that the watchful Superintendent saw no opportunity to taking advantage of it. As the second man turned he recognized him. It was the black man who had almost strangled him.

The man outside swung a leg over the sill and clambered heavily into the room.

'Now,' he said, slamming down the window behind him, 'you two get over in those chairs and I'll fix you so that we shan't have any more trouble.'

'You'll have plenty more trouble,' said Mr. Budd, 'and it'll be bad trouble. What's the idea of this, eh?'

'It's no business of yours,' said the black man. 'You do as you're told!' He made a gesture with the pistol, and with a yawn the stout Superintendent went over to one of the easy chairs and dropped into it.

'Well, it's more comfortable sittin' down I must admit,' he remarked. 'What's the next move?'

'You'll see!' snarled the other man. 'Come on, you! Follow your fat friend,'

Sergeant Leek slouched to the other chair and sat down.

'That's right!' said the man. 'Now we'll have you nice and comfy in a couple of shakes.'

He dragged some odd lengths of rope from his pocket, and advancing began rapidly to secure Mr. Budd's wrists and ankles. When he had rendered the big man completely helpless he turned his attention to Leek and treated him likewise.

'That's all right,' he said, surveying his handiwork. 'You can put that pistol away, Harry.'

The other thrust the weapon into his pocket.

'Now go and put them lights on again,' went on his companion, and the black-faced man hurried away.

Mr. Budd watched the other through half closed eyes. He was of medium height, rather stockily built. A handkerchief had been tied over his face to act as an improvised mask, and he wore a raincoat of some dark material. His voice rather puzzled the Superintendent, for there was something about it that sounded familiar. His memory, however, failed to fit the voice with a name.

'Unlucky you should have come nosing round here tonight,' remarked the man.

'It seems to be,' murmured Mr. Budd, 'and particularly unlucky for my driver. What have you done with his body and the other two people who were here?'

'They're safe enough,' was the answer. 'You needn't worry about them. The killin' of your driver was unfortunate, but

168

it was his own fault. We don't mean no 'arm to the rest of you.'

He raised his hand, inserted his little finger into his right ear and twiddled it rapidly. The action opened a closed cell in Mr. Budd's brain and set free the elusive memory that had bothered him.

'I thought you was in prison, Linman,' he drawled, and the other started violently.

'What d'yer mean?' he demanded. 'You're makin' a mistake, ain't yer? My name's not Linman.'

'It used to be,' said Mr. Budd. 'Maybe you've changed it. It's Barney Linman in police records and it's Barney Linman to me. Thought I recognized your voice.'

At that moment the lights came on again and Mr. Budd blinked in the sudden glare.

'You know too much,' snarled Linman.

'How do you come to be at large?' went on the Superintendent, ignoring the menace in the other's tone. 'The last I heard of you, you were doin' a sentence of five years for burglary with violence.'

'I was released this morning,' growled the man.

Mr. Budd nodded thoughtfully.

'Oh, you were, were you,' he murmured. 'Well, it doesn't look as though it 'ud be long before you were back.'

'You won't put me there,' said Linman. 'There might 'ave been a chance for you if you'd kept yer mouth shut.'

'They hang you for murder in this country,' said Mr. Budd. 'Don't forget that, Barney.'

'They hang yer if they catch yer!' retorted Linman.

'They'll catch you all right,' stated the stout Superintendent. 'Don't you make any mistake about that. Which of you killed Spencer? You or your black friend?'

'Never you mind,' replied Linman. 'By the time we've finished here it won't concern you — nothing 'ull concern you,' he added meaningfully.

He turned as the other man came in, and now that he had an opportunity to see him in the full light for the first time, Mr. Budd realized that he had made a mistake. It was a very natural mistake, for the man's face had been covered with some sort of black stuff, which the stout

Superintendent guessed to be soot.

The reason occurred to him at the same time he made the discovery. He had blacked his face as an elementary effort at disguise, and in the semi-darkness it had proved effectual. Now it was more ludicrous than anything else, suggesting an amateur minstrel performance.

'We can get on with the job now, can't we?' he asked.

'In a minute,' said Linman. 'I'll just search these fellers first.'

'Well, buck up!' said his companion impatiently. 'We've wasted enough time as it is.'

'There's no hurry,' said the other. 'It's only a little after ten and we've got all the night before us.'

The black-faced man growled something below his breath as Linman bent over Mr. Budd and began to search his pockets. He grunted with satisfaction when he found no weapon, and then, as he drew forth the slip of paper and read the scrawled words it contained, his eyebrows, over the handkerchief, drew together.

'What's this?' he demanded.

Mr. Budd shrugged his shoulders.

'Ask your friend,' he answered. 'He dropped it.'

Linman swung round on the man called Harry.

'What's this about?' he asked, and the black-faced man, after a quick glance at the paper, shook his head.

'I dunno!' he declared. 'It don't belong to me. I've never seen it before.'

'He says you dropped it!' snapped Linman.

'Then he's a liar!' retorted the other. 'I don't know nothin' about it!'

'I don't suppose it's very important, anyway,' muttered Linman, and thrust it into his pocket. 'I'll just make sure about this feller and then we'll get on with the job.'

He made a rapid search of Leek's pockets, found nothing, and straightened up.

'Now we can get to work without interruption,' he said, and stopped dead, the breath whistling through his teeth, his eyes glaring at the door.

'What the deuce — ' began the man called Harry as he spun round, but the words froze on his lips, and Mr. Budd, twisting his head, saw the cause.

Standing in the open doorway, motionless, and regarding them steadily, through the veil that covered her face, was the gaunt figure of a woman. Black from head to foot she stood there, her widow's weeds falling over her right shoulder. And then, for the second time that night, all the lights went out!

8

Death in the dark

Linman uttered an oath, and dragging the torch, which he had taken from Mr. Budd out of his pocket pressed the button and sent a ray of light cutting through the darkness in the direction of the doorway.

There was nothing there. The gaunt woman had vanished!

'Did yer see it?' whispered the man called Harry hoarsely. 'My Gawd! A woman all in black!'

'Of course I saw it!' snapped Linman impatiently, and the light jerked spasmodically owing to the shakiness of the hand that held it. 'Go and see who it was!'

'Not bloomin' likely!' said the black-faced man. 'You go yourself!'

'Not afraid of a woman, are you?' sneered his companion. 'Don't be a fool! There's somebody else in this house, and we've gotta find 'em before we can finish what we came for.'

'You find 'em then,' said the other decidedly. 'That wasn't no woman! What would a woman be doin' 'ere on a night like this, eh?'

'What d'you think it was — a ghost?' scoffed Linman.

'I'll take me oath it wasn't nothin' 'uman!' declared Harry firmly. 'Look at the way them lights went out.'

'Well, you put 'em out before, and you're human enough!' snarled Linman. 'I suppose if you could find the main switch somebody else could, couldn't they?'

The man called Harry licked his lips.

'That thing wasn't anywhere near the switch — ' he began nervously.

'Then there must be more than one of 'em,' broke in Linman angrily. 'You don't expect me to believe in spook stuff, do you?'

'I don't care what you believe in!' retorted the black-faced man obstinately. 'You won't get me outside this room, that's flat!

'Oh, very well, I'll go meself!' said the other. 'Give me that pistol.'

Harry dived his hand into his pocket and reluctantly withdrew the weapon.

'What am I goin' to do?' he demanded. 'Supposin' anythin' 'appens — '

'You can have the knife!' snapped Linman, snatching the automatic from his hand. 'You've used it once tonight and you can use it again!'

He went quickly out into the hall, paused for a moment, and then disappeared from view. They saw his shadow, elongated and shapeless, stretch across the floor for an instant, and then that, too, vanished.

The man called Harry stood staring, fascinated, at the dark oblong of the doorway, his breathing irregular and jerky. The sudden appearance of that gaunt, black shape had given him a shock, and Mr. Budd was not surprised. The sight of it standing motionless in the open doorway had sent a cold chill down *his* spine. He remembered the scrawled words on the strip of paper he had found under the rug — the black widow.

Did they refer to this other and unexpected occupant of the house? They were certainly apt. The woman had worn mourning and he had distinctly seen the widow's weeds. But who was she?

The whole thing was very queer. What was Barney Linman and his companion doing in that lonely place on such a night? It seemed to the stout Superintendent that he and Leek had accidentally stumbled into as deep a mystery as they had ever come up against.

He glanced sideways at the melancholy sergeant, and caught his breath, for in the dim light of the dying fire he saw that Leek had got his hands free and was tugging at the knots that secured his ankles.

The black-faced man was still watching the doorway fearfully, and Mr. Budd hoped that he would continue to do so until the lean sergeant had succeeded in releasing himself. The knife, which Linman had suggested the man should use in case of necessity lay where it had dropped on the rug in front of the fireplace. If Leek could take the man called Harry by surprise and gain possession of it —

Mr. Budd almost held his breath as he saw the sergeant straighten up noiselessly from his stooping position. He had succeeded in freeing his ankles!

Without a sound he rose to his feet. But at the same instant something must have warned the black-faced man of his danger, for he swung round. But he was a second too late! One of Leek's long arms went round his neck, jerking up his chin and strangling the cry that rose in his throat. He struggled desperately to free himself, but the sergeant, in spite of his thinness, was as strong as a horse. He clapped one of his hands over the man's mouth to prevent him calling out and giving the alarm to his companion, and then, with a sudden twist, jerked him off his feet, at the same time breaking his fall so that he made little or no noise as he collapsed to the floor. He uttered one hoarse cry, but it was not loud enough to penetrate beyond the room, and before he could utter another Leek had banged his head against the stone fender and knocked him unconscious.

Breathing a little heavily the sergeant staggered to his feet.

'That's settled him!' he whispered, with a note of satisfaction. 'I'll have you free in half a tick.'

'Use the knife,' muttered Mr. Budd, as Leek came towards him with the intention of untying his bonds. 'It'll be quicker.'

The sergeant looked round, saw it, and picking it up came over and slashed through the ropes. The stout Superintendent hoisted himself to his feet ponderously and stretched.

'That's better,' he whispered, and peered down at the limp form of the senseless Harry. 'You must have given him a pretty hefty whack.'

'There wasn't anythin' else I could do,' said Leek.

'That's all right, you needn't apologize,' muttered Mr. Budd. 'It'll probably do him good. Anyway, he won't bother us for a bit.'

'Who was that woman?' said the sergeant below his breath. 'Did you see 'er?'

'Yes, I saw her all right,' grunted Mr.

Budd. 'I dunno her from Eve, except she was better dressed. This house seems to have attracted half the population tonight.

'Linman's gone upstairs,' whispered Leek. 'I 'eard the treads creak.'

'So did I,' answered the Superintendent. 'We'll get him as he comes back. He's sure to return here. You take up a position one side of the door and I'll stand on the other. When he puts his head inside the room we'll get him.'

He moved heavily over as he spoke and Leek followed. Although they listened they could hear nothing from beyond the doorway. An oppressive silence seemed to have settled over the place once more. And then, to their straining ears came a shrill, hoarse scream. It was followed by the sound of a shot, and then an irregular bumping noise that ended in a crash that seemed to shake the whole building.

'My stars, what was that?' whispered Leek, but he whispered it to himself, for Mr. Budd had already vanished into the darkness of the hall.

With his heart in his mouth the lean sergeant followed. It was so dark that he could see nothing but a wall of blackness that seemed like a palpable obstacle in front of him. Instinctively he stretched out his hand and groped his way forward. He trod on something that rolled from under his foot, and stooping he felt about to discover what it was. His fingers touched something smooth and shiny and he guessed it was the torch, which Linman had taken with him when he had gone to seek for the black-clad woman.

He pressed the button and the darkness was dispelled by a beam of light. It lit up the bulky figure of Mr. Budd and something else. Sprawling at the foot of the staircase lay Linman, one knee drawn up and his arms outflung. The handkerchief had slipped from his face, but it was his head that caused Leek to inhale his breath sharply. For the skull was smashed to pulp, and the blood, oozing sluggishly from the terrible wound, was already forming a dark pool on the dusty boards.

9

The legend

Mr. Budd looked down at the sprawling Linman with a frown on his big face. Without a proper medical examination it was difficult to tell whether that dreadful wound had been caused by his fall or by somebody who had struck him heavily over the head. It needed no doctor's opinion, however, to tell him that the man was dead. His position and the expression on his face was sufficient.

The pistol that he had been carrying lay a few yards from the body. The fat detective picked it up. A brief examination showed him that it was fully loaded except for one cartridge, which, from the strong smell of exploded cordite that lingered round the muzzle, had evidently been recently fired.

That must have been the shot they had heard. It was probable that in falling

Linman's finger had involuntarily pressed the trigger. The possession of the weapon was reassuring at any rate. The touch of that cold steel gave a sense of confidence.

He looked up the gloomy staircase. Somewhere in the shadows above lurked the gaunt woman. Was she alone or were there others with her?

Leek, hitherto silent and pale, ventured a question

'What do we do now?' he whispered.

Mr. Budd pursed his fat lips.

'What we ought to do is search the house,' he replied slowly, 'but I'm going to postpone that till later.'

The thin sergeant looked relieved. The idea of going through those dark rooms and shadowy passages after what had occurred did not appeal to him in the least.

'What I'm goin' to do right now,' continued the stout man, 'is look for those Garlands. They're not in the house — I searched it when I found they'd gone, and the only place they can be is in this garage they mentioned. If we can find 'em he'll make a useful addition to our forces.'

'If he's alive,' grunted Leek gloomily. 'Supposin' these people have done 'em in?'

'That's right, be optimistic,' growled Mr. Budd, though the sergeant's suggestion had already crossed his mind. 'You always were a little ray of sunshine.'

'Well,' said Leek, 'it's no good blinkin' facts.'

'Let's wait till it's a fact before we discuss it,' admonished the fat man. 'There's enough trouble round here as it is without imaginin' more. Now, you take this and look after that feller in there' — he jerked his thumb towards the room in which they had left the unconscious Harry — 'and I'll go and have a look see at this garage.'

He stuffed the automatic into Leek's willing hand and moved over to the main door. The fog was as thick as ever, and it was not, he thought, as he surveyed the wall of impenetrable mist, going to be the easiest thing in the world to find the garage at all. He had no idea in which direction it lay, but considered that if he made a circuit of the house he was bound

184

to come on it sooner or later.

Closing the door behind him he descended the steps and set off on his voyage of exploration. The interior of that desolate house was unpleasant enough, but this was, if possible, worse. The fog and the darkness made it difficult to see an inch before him and he stumbled blindly along, pausing every now and again to touch with outstretched hand the wall in order to make sure he was not deviating from his direction.

The torch would have been invaluable, but he had been forced to leave that with Leek. Even if he had waited to find the main switch and put the lights on again there was always the chance that the people still hidden in the place would put them out for purposes of their own, and that would render the sergeant helpless in case of a further attack.

The fog got into his throat and made breathing difficult. The clammy dampness found its way beneath his coat, chilling him, but he kept on. Presently a shadowy something loomed in front of him and he thought he had reached his objective, but it was only an out-building, too small to house anything except a motor cycle. He stopped to examine it, however, and his sense of touch told him that it contained nothing beyond a few garden implements and some old broken boxes.

He continued on his way, rounded a corner of the house and found himself by the back door. Mechanically he tried the handle but the door was locked.

He had completed two sides of the building, and the garage, unless it had been erected at some distance from the place, must be round the next corner. He went on, almost falling over a heap of flowerpots and garden refuse that had been stacked at the side of the narrow path he was traversing. And then he came to the garage.

It had been built on to the side of the house and he had to make a circuit of it before he found the entrance. Judging from the time it took him, he concluded it was a fairly big place. The two heavy doors were shut but he discovered, rather to his surprise, not fastened. He fumbled with the rusty iron staple and tugged.

One leaf of the double door swung slowly outwards and a combined smell of petrol and oil came to his nostrils as he peered into the pitch-black interior. Before entering he felt in his pocket for his matches. There were two left in the box and he had been reserving them for this purpose.

He struck one now, cupping the flame with his hand and cautiously crossed the threshold. The first thing he noticed in the feeble yellow light as the match burnt up was that there was no car. And then he saw the two huddled figures in the far corner and went quickly over to them.

Both Garland and his wife were alive, as their eyes, which gleamed as the light of the match fell on them testified. But they were bound hand and foot and rough gags had been tied around their mouths.

The slither of wood burned down to his fingers and he threw the blackened stump away.

'I'll have you free in a moment,' he said reassuringly, and stooping groped for the knot and untied the gag from the girl's mouth.

He heard her gasp of relief and transferred his attention to the cords at her wrists and ankles, though it was difficult in the dark.

'If you'll light another match,' said the girl hoarsely. 'I'll free Jim.'

Mr. Budd struck his last remaining match and held it while she busied herself with Garland's bonds.

'Thank the Lord for that!' gasped the fair-haired man as he stretched his cramped limbs and staggered to his feet. 'We'd given up hope of being found, and had resigned ourselves to having to spend the night here. Have you got those infernal scoundrels?'

'One of 'em's unconscious and the other's dead,' said Mr. Budd stamping on the end of the used match,

He heard the girl gasp in the darkness.

'Dead?' she whispered.

'Yes,' said the big man. 'But I'm not responsible for that. He was killed by a gaunt woman in widow's weeds who seems also to be lurking about your house.'

'A woman — in widow's weeds?' Garland's voice was incredulous and held a touch of fear. 'Did you see her?'

'I did,' answered Mr. Budd. 'You sound as if you knew her, sir.'

'I know of her. Everybody in the district knows of her,' muttered Garland. 'But I've never met anyone who's ever seen her — Oh, it's impossible!'

'Who is she?' demanded the Superintendent, and there was a perceptible pause before Garland replied,

'She isn't anyone,' he said slowly and surprisingly. 'She — she's a legend — a ghost!'

'A ghost!' Mr. Budd sounded sceptical.

'The Black Widow of Moor Lodge,' said Garland soberly, 'According to the legend to see her means — death.'

10

The stone image

'You're giving me the creeps, Jim,' said the girl petulantly. 'Can't we get out of this place? I'm nearly frozen to death.'

'We'll go back to the house, Nita,' said Garland, 'I'm pretty cold myself.'

'How did you come to be taken by surprise?' asked Mr. Budd, as they all three picked their way across the garage towards the open door.

'It happened soon after you left,' answered Garland. 'Somebody knocked at the door and I thought you'd come back. I went out into the hall, leaving Nita sitting before the fire. I'd barely opened the door when a man sprang at me and knocked me unconscious. I've got a lump on my head the size of a pigeon's egg! When I came to I was trussed up like a chicken. The attack was so sudden that I had no time to draw my automatic.'

'I heard Jim cry out,' put in the girl, 'and came to see what had happened. As I reached the hall somebody caught me by the arm and held a knife at my throat, threatening to kill me if I struggled. The man with the knife was horrible, with a black face — '

'Soot!' broke in Mr. Budd briefly.

'Is that what it was?' said Mrs. Garland. 'Well, he held me till the other man came and tied me up. Then they carried us both out and shut us in the garage.'

'I wonder why they didn't lock the door?' murmured the Superintendent.

'Probably,' said Garland, 'because there wasn't a padlock. I daresay they thought we were safe enough trussed up and gagged. And they were right,' he added. 'We would have been there yet if you hadn't found us.'

So, thought Mr. Budd, that accounted for the fact of his having found the front door open when he had come back after his vain search for Leek and the car. Linman and his companion must have left it open while they took their prisoners round to the garage. They had been there while he had been searching the house.

'I suppose,' he said aloud, 'you don't know these two men, or what their game is?'

'I don't!' answered Garland shortly.

'It's all very interestin' and peculiar,' sighed Mr. Budd. 'I wonder if my sergeant's all right?'

'Don't you expect him to be?' asked the girl apprehensively.

'I don't expect nothin'!' said the big man, shaking his head, 'And I expect anythin'. After what's happened here tonight nothin' 'ud surprise me. I wouldn't even be surprised to find that the whole bloomin' house had vanished.'

'I guess I hope it hasn't,' said the girl. 'It would mean having to go back to that beastly garage.'

They took the shorter way from the garage and reached the house quicker than it had taken Mr. Budd going. At the foot of the steps he remembered something and drew Garland aside.

'That feller Linman 'ull still be in the hall,' he whispered. 'It's not a very pleasant sight. You'd better keep your wife

192

out here for a moment while I cover 'im up.'

'What is it? What are you whispering about?' asked the girl, and Garland told her.

'Oh!' Her voice was dismayed. 'I'd forgotten that. How — how horrible.'

'You won't see anythin' if you let me go in first, Ma'am,' said Mr. Budd reassuringly, and mounting the steps gave a sharp rat-tat on the knocker.

There was a pause, and then the letterbox flap was pushed open from within.

'Who's that?' demanded Leek sharply.

'It's me,' growled Mr. Budd. 'Open the door.'

'What's your Christian name?' said the sergeant.

'Robert!' snarled the Superintendent. 'What d'you think you're doing, canvassing for *Who's Who?*'

The door swung open.

'I wasn't takin' any chances,' explained Leek. 'How was I to know you was you?'

'Who did you think I was, Santa Claus?' said the stout man. 'Get one of

193

the rugs out of the sittin' room and cover up Linman. And don't start arguin',' he added wearily, as Leek's mouth opened to emit the beginning of a question. 'See if you can obey an order for once without.'

He waited by the door until the sergeant had carried out his instructions, and then called the Garlands in. The girl hurried past the ominous looking heap at the foot of the staircase, which showed dimly in the light from the torch in Leek's hand, with averted head and entered the room on the left. The others joined her a moment later.

Mr. Budd looked round for Harry, and discovered that Leek had taken the precaution to tie him up. He had recovered his senses, apparently, but he was evidently still a little dazed.

'Anythin' happened while I've been gone?' asked the Superintendent and Leek shook his head.

'Nothing!' he answered. 'And there ain't been a sound.'

The torch looked a bit dimmer and Mr. Budd suggested that they might find the main switch and put the lights on again.

'It's in a cupboard under the stairs. I'll go,' volunteered Garland.

'Be careful, Jim,' warned his wife anxiously, but he only smiled.

A few seconds after he had left the room the lights came on again and he returned triumphantly.

'That's better!' grunted Mr. Budd. 'Now there are three of us I think we'll make a search of the house for this ghost of yours, Mr. Garland.'

'What's going to happen to me?' asked the girl quickly. 'You're not going to leave me here alone, surely?'

'You'll be quite safe, Ma'am,' said the big man soothingly. 'We'll leave you your husband's pistol. By the way — he took the weapon from Leek's hand — I'm presumin' this is yours.'

Garland looked at it and nodded.

'Yes, that's mine,' he confirmed.

'Well, we'll leave you this pistol,' went on Mr. Budd, 'and if there's any trouble we shall be within earshot.'

'What about him?' she asked, glancing fearfully at the black-faced man.

'He's safe enough,' put in Leek. 'One of

my specialities is tyin' knots.'

'You ought to have been a boy scout!' grunted Mr. Budd. 'Let's go and get this business over, shall we?'

'You won't be long?' said Mrs. Garland anxiously. 'I shall be scared out of my wits until you come back.'

'I suppose,' remarked Garland doubtfully, looking at the sleepy eyed Superintendent, 'that it's essential I should come with you? I mean I hardly like leaving my wife alone and — '

'Very natural,' replied Mr. Budd. 'Well, perhaps you better stay with the lady. It 'ud have been quicker if the three of us went through the house, that's all.'

'I'll come if you wish — ' began Garland, but the fat detective shook his head.

'No, you stay with the lady,' he murmured. 'If we get into any trouble we'll shout.'

He signalled to Leek to accompany him, and went out into the hall.

'You'd better take this back,' he said, pausing at the foot of the staircase and giving the sergeant the automatic. 'I'll take the torch, and then I can do the lookin', and you can do the guardin'.'

'Are we lookin' for that woman?' asked Leek as they began to mount the stairs.

'We're lookin' for anythin' we can find,' answered Mr. Budd.

He reached the first landing and threw the light of the torch to right and to left. Near the wall by the head of the stairs he brought the circle of light to a sudden stop.

'Look at that,' he muttered, pointing, and Leek saw the carved stone figure of a Buddha lying on its side. There was a smear of red on the base.

'That's what finished Linman,' remarked Mr. Budd. 'No wonder his head was smashed like it was. Somebody dropped that from above on him.'

Leek gave a startled glance upward and moved hastily to a safer position.

'You needn't worry,' said the Superintendent. 'I don't suppose there's any more ammunition like that handy. Now, you stand at the head of the stairs and see that nobody gets by while I have a look at these rooms.'

He went through the bedrooms one by one, making a closer examination than he had done before, opening wardrobes and peering under the beds, but he found nothing. The first two were empty.

He was peering with difficulty under the draped bed in the third room when a scream from below startled him.

'Help!' came the girl's voice, shrill and incoherent with terror. 'That woman's got me! The Black Widow. *For God's sake . . .*' There was a choking gurgle and then abruptly the cries ceased!

11

More mystery

'What's the matter? What's happened?'

Mr. Budd heard Leek's voice shouting as he scrambled ponderously to his feet, and the sergeant's heavy steps went thudding down the stairs. He moved quickly to the door, but as he reached it, it was jerked shut with a bang and the key clicked in the lock.

'Who's there? Let me out!' he demanded, but his only reply was a little chuckle that came faintly to his ears from the other side of the door.

He turned his light on the lock. It was heavy and old-fashioned. The door itself was of thick, well-seasoned oak, and he concluded that nothing short of a battering ram or a dynamite charge would break down the barrier.

He was a prisoner!

He compressed his lips and gently

caressed his cascade of chins. Faintly to his ears came the sound of excited voices from downstairs, followed by a shot, then silence.

Mr. Budd frowned. Who had locked him in? Someone who had been lurking in the darkness of the landing, or more likely on the stairs leading to the upper floor. Someone who had awaited their opportunity and taken advantage of it when Leek's attention was distracted by Mrs. Garland's scream from below.

He hammered on the door loudly and shouted, but no one took any notice of him. Except for the din he himself was making the house was completely silent.

Panting, he gave up his efforts after a moment or two, and searched round for something more substantial with which to attack the door. By the side of the big bed was a heavily constructed oak table, and, seizing this by the legs, Mr. Budd rained blow after blow on the panels, but they withstood his onslaught. The table was heavy and after a little while he was forced to rest. Setting it down he pulled out his torch and with its light examined the door to see what damage he had done. Beyond denting the woodwork he had made no appreciable impression on that solid barrier.

Wiping the perspiration from his forehead with the back of his hand he went over to the window, raised the sash, and peered out. The ground was invisible, shrouded in fog, but he directed his light down the side of the house in the hope that he might find something that would enable him to escape this way. There was nothing, neither creeper nor drainpipe. The wall fell sheer below him, vanishing into the mist.

He returned to the door and listened. Absolute stillness greeted his ears. What had happened to the people downstairs? Had they succumbed to this unexpected attack, which had caught him unawares? Unless they had they must have heard the row he had been making. Leek, at any rate, would have come up to discover tbe cause. The only conclusion to be drawn was that the thin sergeant was incapable of investigating, which meant that he and the Garlands had been overpowered. By whom? By the gaunt woman who was playing ghosts? It was next to impossible, for even if it was a man masquerading, he could not have successfully tackled three people single handed, and one armed at that. Which suggested that there were other people in the house as well.

Mr. Budd rubbed the side of his nose irritably. How many had come to this lonely house under cover of the fog, and what in the world was at the bottom of it? Obviously these other people, whoever they were, had no connection with Linman and the man called Harry, otherwise Linman would not have been so startled at the apparition of the gaunt woman, nor would he have been killed.

Moor Lodge was evidently the focal point of some very queer and extraordinary business, but what it was Mr. Budd was forced to admit he hadn't the least idea.

Breathing more normally, and considerably rested, he began to consider his next move. It seemed to be purely a waste of time to try and break open the door, and escape by the window appeared to be equally futile. Since there was no other outlet to the room it looked, on the face of it, as if he would have to remain where he was. But this didn't appeal to him at all. He was intensely anxious to find out what had happened downstairs.

Sitting on the edge of the bed he wrinkled his broad forehead in an effort to evolve some plan, but he could think of nothing practicable. He sighed wearily. He had had a long day and he was both tired and hungry, a state that was not conducive to clear thought.

He eyed the dusty hangings of the bed and made a wry grimace. He had read in a book once how a man in a similar position to his own had escaped by making a rope out of sheets, and climbed down from the window.

'I'll bet he didn't weigh sixteen stone!' muttered Mr. Budd, to himself, ruefully. 'So *that's* ruled out.'

Neither were there likely to be any secret panels. That was another thing that only happened in fiction, although these ancient walls of carved oak looked as if they might conceal half a dozen such things. It was improbable there would be anything of the sort, but there might be . . .

He stared slowly round the apartment. The house was undoubtedly very old, and in old houses secret passages with entrances in various rooms had been found . . .

He got up, smiling at his optimism, and began an inspection of the worm-eaten panelled walls. He told himself it was a waste of time, but until he could find someway of getting out of that room he had plenty of time to waste, and he might just as well waste it that way as any other.

Starting at the door he went slowly round the big apartment examining, tapping, sounding, but all to no purpose. There was not even a place where the woodwork sounded hollow to reward his diligence He came to the wall beside the massive four-poster bed His light was growing very dim by now the overworked battery was giving out. The wall here sounded as solid as the others, and although he had expected nothing else he was conscious of a slight feeling of disappointment.

He was turning away from his unpro-
ductive labours to round the bed and
examine the last remaining patch of wall
on the other side when his foot caught in
the ancient rug on the floor and he
tripped. To save himself from falling he
flung out his arm and clutched at the
wall. His fingers slid over the carved oak
and something went click.

A panel the size of a small cupboard
swung out an inch. Mr. Budd, his usually
sleepy eyes wide with excitement, pulled
it fully open and shone his light into the
box-like apartment that it had concealed.

It was packed with wash-leather bags of
varying size. He pulled them out one after
the other, piling them on the bed, and
when he had removed the last began to
open them.

As he saw the contents of the first he
drew in his breath sharply, and when they
were all open stared dumbfounded.

Heaped on the bed was a glittering
mass: hundreds of unset diamonds
representing a fortune running into many
thousands of pounds.

Mr. Budd stared at the treasure he had

accidentally unearthed, his mouth open and his eyes wide. No longer was there any reason for him to ask himself what lay behind the extraordinary popularity of that old house on this foggy night. There was his answer before his eyes. Linman, the man called Harry, and the other mysterious people were all after those sparkling stones. That was as obvious as the stones themselves.

But how had they come to be where he had found them in the first place? For they were the proceeds of the robbery at Mornington's, the robbery for which Charles Wenham was now serving a sentence in Princetown Convict Prison, and the reason which had brought Mr. Budd to this part of the world at all.

Had Wenham hidden them there before he was arrested?

The fat detective drew his brows together. Something James Garland had said recurred to him, something about the house having been let to a man called Kingsley, who had died there — when was it he had died? Three years ago. That was it, he remembered now. Three years ago, and he had occupied the house three years prior to his death. Mr. Budd made a rapid calculation. He would have been living there at the time of the robbery, so unless Wenham knew him and they had acted in collusion he would have had no opportunity for hiding the diamonds before his arrest.

That must be the explanation of it. Kingsley had been an accomplice of Wenham's. The man had died three years before these people who were searching had become aware of the existence of the diamonds. But why had such a long time elapsed? Why hadn't they known about them before?

Mr. Budd considered this carefully, but could not find an answer to satisfy him, and turned his attention to Linman's part in the affair.

Linman had, on his own confession, been released from the prison that morning; the prison where Charles Wenham was lying ill with lobar pneumonia. Every crook big and small, knew of the Mornington Robbery. It had been front-page news in its day and was still talked about. It was publicly known, too, that the proceeds had never been recovered. Had Wenham during a bout of delirium, mentioned where these were hidden, and had Linman overheard him?

Mr. Budd tried to think how this could be possible. How could Linman overhear him? Wenham was in the infirmary How could Linman — yes, there was a way by which Linman could have been present if Wenham had said anything about the whereabouts of the stones; a way that was quite likely and possible. He could have been the hospital orderly. It was more than likely he would, since his sentence was nearly up be put on to light duty.

It fitted! Mr. Budd was pretty certain that he had settled Linman's place in the scheme of things. But what about Harry? How did the black-faced man come into it? He was obviously a friend of the dead ex-convict. Probably Linman, when he had left the prison that morning, had gone up to London, searched out his friend and together they had come down to seek for the hidden stones.

The mystery was beginning to clear. He

felt that if he wasn't completely right he was as near it as didn't matter very much. They had come down expecting to find an empty house, for on the morning when Linman had been released the house had been empty, he had possibly made inquiries in the district and discovered that. They had come down expecting to find an empty house and had found — the Garlands.

That must have been rather a shock. It was, of course, the black-faced man or Linman whom Mrs. Garland had seen at the window, and it was definitely Harry who had killed Spencer.

So far Mr. Budd was able to theorise without difficulty. But now he came up against the other and more mysterious people. Who was the person in the widow's weeds whom he had glimpsed in the doorway? Who was the person who had killed Linman, and how had they got to learn of the whereabouts of the diamonds?

This was frankly unanswerable. In the case of Linman and his companion he had had a lead, but here there was nothing to go on.

Mr. Budd began to scoop the gems up in his palm and put them back in the little bags. When he had done this and restored them to the compartment behind the panel he turned his attention to his most immediate difficulty, and that was to get out of that room.

Once more he went over to the door and listened but no sound at all readied his ears. He was in the act of picking up the table with the intention of trying a fresh onslaught on the door when a noise in the direction of the window attracted his attention. He whirled round sharply and in the now feeble glimmer of his torch saw the top of a ladder appear against the sill.

He had left the sash open, and as he watched, expecting an attack, he saw the ladder quiver. Presently a man's head and shoulders appeared. Through the blood that streaked the white face he recognized him. It was Sergeant Leek!

12

Mr. Budd trumps the ace

Mr. Budd went quickly over to the window. Leek was the last person he had expected to see.

'Quick,' whispered the sergeant hoarsely, before he could speak. 'Follow me down the ladder. I saw the light in this winder an' guessed you was up here.'

He began to descend, rung by rung, almost before he had completed his last sentence. The stout man, after a momentary hesitation, swung his leg over the sill, felt gingerly with his foot for a hold, and started to follow him. The ladder swayed unpleasantly under his weight, but in a few minutes he found himself standing on firm ground by the side of his lean subordinate.

'What happened?' he asked in a low voice.

'It's too long to tell you now,' replied

Leek. 'Come on.'

'Where are we going?' asked the fat Superintendent.

'I want to show you something,' said the sergeant.

For once the roles were reversed and it was Leek who took the lead. Mr. Budd followed him slowly as they made their way with difficulty through the fog round an angle of the house. Presently they came to the lighted window of the sitting room. Leek placed his hand on his superior's arm and applying his lips close to his ear whispered:

'Don't make a sound!'

He tiptoed forward with Mr. Budd at his heels and presently the stout man was able to peer in through the window.

The black-faced man had disappeared and James Garland and his wife were the sole occupants of the room. But they were not prisoners, they were very active indeed! Garland was on his hands and knees carefully examining the floor, and the girl was busy searching the various articles of furniture.

As Mr. Budd looked she began ripping

open the seat of a chair with the blade of a clasp knife. He watched her search feverishly amongst the padding, and saw the look of disappointment on her face when she found nothing. He knew what she was looking for, and knew now who had been the second lot of people in this business. There were several details to straighten out, but the main issue was as clear as day.

His immediate problem was how to take these two by surprise.

He drew Leek away from the window and out of possible earshot.

'I suppose they took the revolver from you?' he whispered.

The sergeant nodded.

'Yes,' he replied. 'When I ran downstairs to see why the woman had screamed I found her in that room by herself. She was staring at the window, which was open. I didn't suspect anythin'. That woman! She gasped, and pointed, and I went over. There was nothin' there, and when I put me head out somebody clubbed me. I don't remember nothin' more except hearin' the pistol explode as it fell from my hand. When I came to meself I was in the kitchen with the doors locked, but they'd forgotten a small pantry with a tiny window. It was very small, and it took me all me time to squeeze through it, but I managed it. I made me way round to the window and saw those two pullin' the furniture about and tappin' the walls. I knew then who had been responsible for coshin' me.'

Mr. Budd nodded.

'Garland, of course,' he muttered. 'The woman's scream was a fake. What d'you do then?'

'I thought the best thin' to do,' said the sergeant, 'was to try and find you. I didn't know what 'ad 'appened to you, but when I looked up at the house I could just make out, through the fog, a light in one of the windows. I guessed then that that's where you was, and I was making me way round the 'ouse to try and find some means of gettin' in so that I could creep up the stairs when I saw a ladder reared up against a window at the back.'

'It wasn't there when I was tryin' to find the garage,' muttered Mr. Budd, and then a light broke on him. 'Of course, it was the way Garland got in and was able to lock that door on me without passin' you. Go on.'

'I carried the ladder back to the window which was lighted,' continued the sergeant, 'and the rest you know.'

'H'm!' grunted Mr. Budd. 'The question is at the moment what are we goin' to do? That feller's armed. We don't stand much chance against an automatic.'

The sergeant scratched his head, but he could offer no solution. His activities of the night had drained him of all further initiative.

'Listen!' said the stout man after an interval. 'If we can get hold of Garland, and that gun, the woman should be easy.'

'But how are we goin' to do it?' muttered Leek.

'I'll tell you,' Mr. Budd spoke rapidly. 'D'you think you can wail?'

'What?' gasped the astonished Leek.

'Wail!' repeated the Superintendent impatiently. 'Howl! Make some sort of extraordinary noise outside here that's likely to bring Garland to the door to investigate.'

'I should think so,' said Leek. 'I used to sing in the choir when I was a boy — '

'That ought to be extraordinary enough!' grunted Mr. Budd. 'If you can do that I'll conceal meself at one side of the porch with a stick and we'll get him.'

The sergeant was a little doubtful, but his superior overruled his objections.

'Let's see if we can find a stick,' he said, and began searching about in the fog.

It was some time before he found what he wanted, a heavy baulk of timber that at one time had formed part of the pergola. Armed with this he issued final instructions to Leek and crept round to the front entrance. There was ample room for him to take up his position at one side of the door.

He waited. Presently, out of the mist-swathed night, came a most appalling noise; a thin wail of sound that swelled into a scream and ended in a throaty gurgle. Mr. Budd shuddered.

There was a pause, and then Leek repeated his efforts, an even more dreadful canto than before.

A sound of movement in the hall

216

reached Mr. Budd's ears and he stiffened. Footsteps came to the other side of the door, stopped, and then it was flung open and Garland appeared, the automatic gripped in his hand.

He peered out into the fog, advanced a step, and Mr. Budd took a firmer grasp of his weapon. The heavy stick rose, whistled through the air as it descended, and caught Garland full on his pistol wrist.

He gave a yell of pain and the automatic flew from his hand. At the same instant Mr. Budd sprang forward, wound his arms round the man's waist, and jerked him off his feet.

'Come on, Leek!' he panted, and the lean figure of the sergeant emerged from the mist.

'Pick up his pistol,' gasped the stout man as he strove desperately to subdue the writhing figure beneath him.

Leek stooped, searched for it, and straightened with it in his hand just as the girl appeared.

Mr. Budd released his hold and scrambled up.

'Now keep still,' he said. 'Sergeant

Leek's covering you, and if you try any funny tricks he'll shoot! I've had enough nonsense this evenin' to be goin' on with.'

Garland sat up, rubbing his throat, and the girl screamed.

'And you keep quiet, too!' said Mr. Budd irritably. 'This is the end o'your picnic.'

He took the pistol from Leek's hand and covered them.

'Get up!' he said to Garland, and when the man staggered to his feet waved him back into the hall.

'What — ' began Garland thickly, but the fat detective interrupted him.

'You don' want to say nothin',' he said. 'You just keep quiet. You'll have plenty of opportunity for makin' statements later.'

'What are you going to do with us?' asked the girl.

'I'm goin' to tie you both up so that you can't move,' said Mr. Budd, 'and then Leek and I are goin' to make a meal from that food I saw in the kitchen on the table, and wait in peace and quietness until the fog clears in the mornin'. I think we've earned both.'

With a squeaking of brakes Mr. Budd brought the police car to a halt in front of the police station at Tavistock and Sergeant Leek got down from the seat beside his superior and entered the building. After a short interval he reappeared, accompanied by an astonished Inspector and a constable.

'Sergeant Leek has made an extraordinary statement,' said the local man.

'And I'm goin' to make another!' broke in the fat Superintendent. 'You'll find two men and a woman in the back of this car. Take 'em inside and lock 'em safely up. There's a charge of murder against the two men, and one of accessory before and after the fact against the woman. I'll come in and make the charge.'

At a sign from the Inspector the constable pulled open the door, and with the assistance of Leek dragged out the three helpless prisoners.

'What's this bundle, sir?' asked the policeman, pointing to a bulky package lying on the floor.

'You can leave that where it is,' said Mr. Budd. 'It's worth, accordin' to its owners, about two hundred and fifty thousand pounds!'

He clambered laboriously down from behind the wheel.

'While you're getting' ready for me to charge these people,' he said, 'I'd like to put through a call to the Gov'nor of Princetown Prison.'

★ ★ ★

'Good Heavens, what an extraordinary story!' exclaimed the Assistant Commissioner later that evening, staring across his littered desk at the sleepy-eyed man who overflowed the chair before him. 'What happened after you succeeded in capturing these Garlands?'

'Their name isn't Garland,' said Mr. Budd, 'but I'll come to that presently. After Leek had tied 'em up and we'd made certain they were secure, we had a good meal and spent the rest of the night alternately dozing. The fog had cleared off by the mornin' and I went out to see if I could find what had happened to the car and Spencer's body. I found 'em both hidden in a little wood that was part of the grounds belonging to Moor Lodge. This black-faced feller, Harry Cann, says it was Linman's idea to hide the car so as they could use it after they'd found the diamonds for a getaway.'

'That's the man who killed Spencer?' said Colonel Blair, and Mr. Budd nodded.

'Yes,' he answered. 'Spencer came upon him at the gate of Moor Lodge talkin' to Linman. They was discussin' what they should do now they'd unexpectedly found the house which should have been empty occupied, and they mentioned the diamonds. Spencer foolishly let 'em know he'd overheard what they were talkin' about, and Cann killed him to prevent him comin' back and splittin' to us. Spencer had said who he was and that we were in the vicinity. He didn't know who the men were, but he caught sight of Cann's black face and I suppose he thought he was coloured. That's what he was tryin' to tell me when he died.'

'How do these other people come into it?' demanded the Assistant Commissioner frowning. 'You say their names aren't Garland?'

'No, sir,' said Mr. Budd. 'Their name's Kingsley, Mr. and Mrs. Kingsley. He's the son of the man who died in Moor Lodge three years ago, the man who was behind Wenham in the Mornington Robbery. He was a sort of fence, but there was such a hue and cry out at that time that he was holdin' up tryin' to find a market for the stones until it had died down a bit. Unluckily for him he died before he could do anythin' about it. His son, this feller James Garland as he calls himself, was a pretty bad hat, and was in prison in America at the time of his father's death, and he didn't know nothin' about the existence of these diamonds until after his release when he landed in England the day before yesterday with his wife and visited old Kingsley's solicitor. The old man had left a letter for him which, being too weak to write himself he had dictated to the doctor who attended him, which, of course, meant that he had to be guarded in what he said. Leonard Kingsley had done a lot of business for his father and knew about him being a fence. The old man shipped a lot of the stuff he got hold of abroad for his son to market, and in the correspondence that passed between 'em they used various commonplace names, which meant somethin' quite different. In this way the old man was able in this letter to tell his son that the diamonds was in the house, but not where.

'He'd 'ave had to use plain English to describe the panel, and he couldn't do it. The lease which he had taken hadn't run out and so the solicitor, I've seen him by the way, was quite willin' to hand over the key of Moor Lodge to this feller, Leonard Kingsley. He also mentioned to him in the course of conversation the legend connected with the property, the Black Widow, which was supposed to appear when death threatened the family — the usual stuff.

'It gave Kingsley, however, an idea, because he didn't know there was goin' to be a fog, and he thought that if some passin' cottager or other inquisitive person saw a light and wanted to investigate too closely the sight of the Black Widow 'ud scare 'em off. He noted the name on a scrap of paper, which I found under the rug in the sittin' room, and hired the costume which he used after from one of the theatrical costumiers.'

'Astounding!' murmured the Assistant Commissioner. 'Why did he call himself Garland?'

'Because Garland is the name of the real owner of Moor Lodge,' said Mr. Budd, 'and he's really somewhere abroad. I learned that from the solicitor, too. In fact he was all timed to go down and make a search for these diamonds when two unexpected things upset his calculations. First Linman, who had been an orderly at the infirmary in the prison and overheard Wenham talking about the house and the diamonds in his delirium, turned up with his pal, and secondly when I put in an appearance.'

'And you say,' said Colonel Blair, 'that it was Garland, or Kingsley, who adopted the disguise of the gaunt woman. How was that when you found them bound and gagged in the garage after the death of Linman?'

'He *had* been bound and gagged,' explained Mr. Budd. 'Linman and Cann did that after coshing him. But he managed to get free, and entered the house by the back door with the girl. His widow get-up was in the kitchen, and he only had to slip it on before appearin' in the doorway.'

'Why did he bother?' asked Colonel Blair.

'He wanted to hear what we was sayin', and find out who Linman and the other feller was. He didn't know that, and he didn't want me and Leek to know he was anythin' but what he said. That's why, after droppin' that image on Linman's head and hearin' me arrange to go round and search the garage he waited till we'd gone, slipped out of his widow's get-up, let himself out by the back door and went back to the garage with his wife and tied himself up. It wasn't difficult. He tied her first then himself, that's why she was so anxious to release him so that I shouldn't find out how loosely the cords were bound about his wrists.'

'Well, you certainly had an excitin' time,' said the Assistant Commissioner. 'And you never saw Wenham after all?'

'I wouldn't have done any good seein' him, anyway,' answered Mr. Budd. 'He died just as we got stuck in the fog.'

'Well it was lucky you did, after all,' remarked Colonel Blair. 'Otherwise we'd never have found those diamonds, and these people's little game wouldn't have been nipped in the bud.'

'By the Budd, sir,' corrected the stout Superintendent complacently, and the Assistant Commissioner smiled.

THE END